CLOUDWISH

CLOUDWISH

FIONA WOOD

POPPY
Little, Brown and Company
New York   Boston

ALSO BY FIONA WOOD
Six Impossible Things
Wildlife

Poppy

Hachette Book Group
1290 Avenue of the Americas, New York, NY 10104
Visit us at lb-teens.com

Poppy is an imprint of Little, Brown and Company.
The Poppy name and logo are trademarks of Hachette Book Group, Inc.

The publisher is not responsible for websites (or their content) that are not owned by the publisher.

First U.S. Edition: October 2016
First published in 2015 by Pan Macmillan Australia PTY, Ltd.

Library of Congress Cataloging-in-Publication Data
Names: Wood, Fiona (Fiona Anna) author.
Title: Cloudwish / by Fiona Wood.
Description: First U.S. edition. | New York ; Boston : Little, Brown and Company, 2016. | "Poppy." | "First published in 2015 by Pan Macmillan Australia PTY, Ltd." | Summary: "Vietnamese-Australian teenager Vân Ước Phan, the daughter of Vietnamese immigrants, doesn't believe in magic until the day an absentminded wish actually comes true and she attracts the attention of her longtime crush." —Provided by publisher.
Identifiers: LCCN 2015036989| ISBN 9780316242127 (hc) | ISBN 9780316242110 (ebook)
Subjects: LCSH: Vietnamese—Australia—Juvenile fiction. | CYAC: Vietnamese—Australia—Fiction. | Dating (Social life and customs)—Fiction. | Wishes—Fiction. | Magic—Fiction. | Australia—Fiction.
Classification: LCC PZ7.W84925 Cl 2016 | DDC [Fic]—dc23
LC record available at http://lccn.loc.gov/2015036989

10 9 8 7 6 5 4 3 2 1

LSC-C

Printed in the United States of America

For the students and tutors of Friday Night School, past and present

I recognized myself in *Jane Eyre*. It amazes me how many white people can't read themselves in black characters. I didn't feel any separation between me and Jane. We were tight.

ALICE WALKER
Sydney Writers' Festival, 2014

1

At home, this was her own private view of the world: grimy, tiny, vast. Her go-to hallway window. A fixed glass plate, exactly twenty-six by thirty-two inches. She used to stand on tiptoes to see through it, and every night it turned the city into an electric fairyland. Once upon a long time ago she believed in magic.

• • •

A creative writing master class on the first day back? They weren't kidding with the whole pep talk about hitting the ground running this year. The visiting writer, Ronette Bartloch—it had to be a pen name—was wittering about fantasy. She invited them to interpret fantasy as broadly as they liked—*thanks, heaps*—from fairy tale to political manifesto. She spoke in such a low, humming voice it was almost impossible to tune in at the dozy end of the day.

For Vân Ước, fantasies fell into two categories: nourishing or pointless.

Daydreaming about Billy Gardiner, for example? Pointless. It always left her feeling sick, as though she'd eaten too much sugar. And there was zero chance of a payoff, because she had observed Billy Gardiner in his native habitat for two years now, and it was a truth universally acknowledged that he only ever went out with girls like Pippa or Tiff or Ava. Foreground, high-resolution girls. And, even then, not for long.

Buzz around the lockers was that he'd hooked up with Holly at a couple of parties over the summer break.

Vân Ước allowed herself a covert sideways glance at the boy in question. Right across the aisle. Close enough to touch. Stretching back in his chair, oar-calloused hands clasped over the back of his messy blond hair, shirtsleeves rolled up, sharp forearm flexors. His nose in profile, relative to forehead and chin, must be one of those precise proportions that define visual harmony. The golden mean. She smiled as she imagined measuring his face to check it. His eyes were closed. Concentrating? Dozing? He was probably on the river rowing by five thirty this morning...

A nourishing fantasy, on the other hand, was okay as long as you didn't indulge just before bedtime, or you could end up with your nose pressed so close to what you hoped for that sleep wouldn't have a chance.

So, daydreaming about being at her own art exhibition opening? Nourishing. She could see it, taste it, frame after delicious frame. Her dramatic, large-scale work of minutely beautiful things, the artsy yet fashionable crowd. Her modest thanks at the praise being poured over her like honey. *No, really… Too, too kind…* The flash of cameras. Clothes… something fluidly androgynous, directional, by a Japanese designer. In a slatey gray. Billy Gardiner *wishing* he'd gotten to know her when they were at school together. *Kicking himself* that he hadn't.

In the most lock-and-key part of her dreamscape, she believed the art thing might conceivably happen. Minus the Billy Gardiner element. If she worked hard enough. Maybe.

Thankfully, the nature of fantasy was private. Because her parents must never guess. Because in *their* fantasies she was a doctor. White coat. Stethoscope. Large income. Comfortable retirement for the whole family. A big house in their dream suburb, Kew. (Why the obsession with Kew?)

Little hitch.

Little inconsistency re dreamsgoalsdesiredoutcomes.

So that was one door of the nourishing fantasy that was better kept shut. Behind that door stood her mother and father, her hardworking, first-generation-immigrant, barely-English-speaking Vietnamese Australian parents screaming *noooooooooooo* in a horror film slo-mo reaction shot. And then attacking her with blunt instruments.

She took a calming breath. Still plenty of school to get through before she needed to face hand-to-hand combat with her parents over university course selection. This was only the first week of the two-year International Baccalaureate (IB) program at Crowthorne Grammar, where she had been at school since year nine.

Anyway, she limited the wishing, dreaming, fantasy activities, too pragmatic to let them take over. She preferred things that could be proved, or held. The plastic fantastic—the trustworthy, physical world. Physics. Chemistry. Art. Most of all, art.

She rested her hands in her lap, doing a couple of the gentle stretches the doctor had given her to do after diagnosing repetitive strain injury last year. At the time she was devastated because it meant having to change media from her flick-stroke, photorealist drawings to actual photography for her IB portfolio. Like drummers, people who draw are notoriously fidgety; she missed the pencil in her hand like a ghost limb, and still felt the twitch of its absence. Fortunately, her camera was grafting itself to her hand quite comfortably.

Enthused and pink-cheeked, in witchy ankle boots and a retro sundress, Ms. Bartloch was encouraging the class to select from her box of creative prompts.

Their challenge for the fantasy class was to imagine things as they might be, not as they were. To let themselves be transported to another place or time.

Holly Broderick was talking about a friend's penthouse apartment in the city that sure was *her* idea of fantasy. That girl was the perfectly formed love child of Smirk and Snarl. She spent half her time showing off and the other half looking for someone to squash. Holly was not as pretty as Ava, not as

4

rich as Pippa, not as "Establishment" as Gabi, but boy did she rule at being mean. If she were ever to feel the full force of Vân Ước's dislike, she'd probably fall over and never get up again. It was easier to avoid eye contact altogether than cause possible mortal injury, even to someone as deserving of it as Holly.

Why did these days at the beginning of the year go so slowly, when by the end of term they rushed along at warp speed? Was it only six hours ago she'd slipped into her mother-ironed summer uniform and looked out at her very own million-dollar view toward the bay? Although—penthouse apartment in Melbourne? Make that a two-, maybe three-million-dollar view. Real estate was getting ridiculous.

Not that her parents paid market rates for their view. It was courtesy of the state government. Low-rent, high-rise, run-down public housing. She was the only girl in her class who lived in a place like that. But the view was great. What you could see of it anyway, out of small aluminum-framed windows with years' worth of grime on the outside.

By the time the fantasy-prompt box made its way to Vân Ước, all the interesting stuff was taken. On surrounding desktops she saw an assortment of little plastic dolls and cars, exotic feathers, old coins, a couple of tarot cards, china fragments, and even some bones. She fished about. A few crappy shells and the obligatory vintage postcards were all that was left. Classic. The meek shall inherit the dregs.

She hated creative writing. It was her least favorite aspect of English, and she had probably already written in advance enough pieces to cover her in this area. Summer hadn't been

5

exactly oversubscribed in the social department. There was plenty of preparation time for this year's work.

Ms. Bartloch came over, stirred her hand through the box, and offered it to Vân Ước again. A glass vial peeped out from under the postcards. That looked a bit more interesting. She examined it at close range: a little tube of glass, each end sealed with a twist. Inside, a floating slip of paper on which one word was written in spidery faded ink: *wish*.

The vial warmed to blood temperature in her hand as she free-associated with the chosen item, as they'd been instructed to do. *Wish* led straight to Billy Gardiner, naturally. In a different world, she might belong here. She would not live in the dumpbin category of scholarship/poor/smart/Asian. She'd be one of the guys. Plenty of the "guys" *were* Asian, of course; it was a diverse community. But, unlike Vân Ước, they were from backgrounds of privilege: corporate expats' kids or second- and third-generation locals.

She imagined having money in her pocket for after-school coffees on Greville Street. At leisure all weekend simply to hang out. Stories to swap about her latest holiday. A family she'd feel relaxed enough about to take for granted, even to bitch about occasionally. And a boy like Billy Gardiner. She had permission—instruction—to wish. Sugar high and depressing comedown on the horizon. Deep breath. She wished, with a quick, hard ache of impossibility, that Billy Gardiner liked her. More than liked her. Preferred her to all the other girls in the school. All the other girls in the world. Found her...*fascinating*.

"Everyone writing something, please," Ms. Bartloch was saying, looking at her watch. Her tone was so annoying, like someone leading a meditation. And, embarrassingly, she had her eyes shut. "Start with some free writing...let the words flow...open yourself to your theme...welcome any ideas that come to you...don't think of spelling or grammar...remember the wonderful *Select All/Delete*—your limbering up is completely free, completely private."

Looking around, Vân Ước realized with an uncomfortable heart thump that she was the only person not tapping away on her keyboard. Coming last—at anything, even free writing—was not an option.

Cue the idiot life commentators. They lived, uninvited, on the doorstep of all her inadequacies: two of them, old white dudes, heckling as they watched her every hesitation, every failure: *Yes, the scholarship girl has dropped the ball/Will the visiting writer mention her tardiness in the staffroom?/It's certainly possible/Possible? It's a sure thing! Vân Ước Phan needs to pick up her game if she's planning to go the distance.*

She uncurled her fingers to take one more look at the glass vial, but it was gone. It must have slipped from her hand while she was in Billy-zone. She looked in her lap. She bent down, scanning the floor under her desk. Checked under her chair. Under the desk in front of her. The desk behind her. Inside her pencil case. Emptied her pencil case. Dropped things from her pencil case on the floor. She was growing hot with discomfort. The teacher might think she'd stolen it—the constant worry of the poorest kid in the room. Where the hell was it?

Everyone seemed busy writing. So she risked standing up. Surely it couldn't have slipped inside her dress. She stood up, pulled her dress out at the front, looked down, shook herself as discreetly as possible. A quick shimmy. A little hop. But nothing fell out.

"Lost something?" Billy Gardiner was looking at her oddly. No wonder. He'd obviously witnessed the whole bend-and-stretch routine. He leaned down and picked up a pen. "This?"

"No." She took the pen. "But thanks."

She put up her hand and witchy boots came over. "I'm so sorry. I've somehow misplaced the little…" Vân Ước held her fingers up, vial distance apart.

Ms. Bartloch nodded, then whispered so as not to distract the other students. "Don't worry—sorry, what's your name?"

Flustered, Vân Ước said her name with correct Vietnamese pronunciation, the lilting double vowel and upward inflection on "Ước." She registered Ms. Bartloch not quite catching the pronunciation, and repeated it with the Anglo flatness she used for school, because everyone could manage it: *Van Oc.*

"Things wander from that box and find their way back, Vân Ước."

"But I've looked everywhere."

"Better get started, anyway—I promised Ms. Norton you'd all have something to go on with after this session."

Okay—free writing—free freeeeeeeee meeeee youuuuu blah blah wish theme fantasy wish fish delish wish mish kish pish quish squish what will I write I write the write right wrong free to enter wish wish wish I wish I wish I hadn't read the article about the fucking government's new legislation on boat people how dare they how dare they stand in the fortress the high places the towers of privilege stamp down rain down reign down on the people who can't find the first foothold in the green water floating drowning the soft sand the sand too far too far far far below never making it to shore they are no different from us us and them us is them we are them them and us them us them us them us wish us them them wish us out okay limbered.

Select All. Delete.

Creative Prompt: The word "Wish." Vân Ước Phan. English: 11015EN(N).

The wish many of us share is simple to express but, it seems, hard to achieve: we want a just and equitable society, one that welcomes those seeking asylum from political and religious persecution. My parents found such a society when they arrived by boat in Australia from Vietnam in 1980. The intervening years have seen sympathy waning, and opposing governments have come to office in recent years partly on the bipartisan, and, sadly, popular platform of "Keep out the boats." I wish for a different...

Half an hour raced by in a burst of political outrage. How dare this government describe asylum seekers who arrived by boat as "illegals," deliberately misinforming the electorate?

Her parents' generation was given asylum after the fall of Saigon, people from Europe were given asylum after the Second World War, and now there were detention centers like Manus Island and Nauru, where *kids* from places like Iraq and Afghanistan were imprisoned. This had turned into a country that didn't care about its humanitarian responsibilities. What had happened?

As she wrote, she tried to evoke the fear and desperation that people must feel in order to risk traveling in this way, imperiling themselves and their family.

Billy Gardiner did not make an appearance.

Did everyone live this kind of double life?

• • •

Packing up to go home by the lockers after her oboe class, she saw that the only other person still around was Billy Gardiner. And he appeared to be staring at her.

"So, did you find it?"

He couldn't be speaking to her. Billy Gardiner did not seek out Vân Ước Phan for after-school chitchat.

He came a couple of steps closer. He was buzzing. He pulled the phone from his pocket, glanced at the screen, switched it off, stuffed it back in. "Whatever you thought was inside your dress—did you find it?" He was smiling the question. Had put her ahead of the phone call in his queue of popular-boy activities. Was looking at her with complete attention. Not the *sorry, I bumped you on the way past* look, not the *scanning the crowd and not bothering to stop* look, not the *don't really know who you are* look. But eye to eye. Waiting. Listening.

"No," she said. "No, I didn't." And walked off.

Nice one, Vân Ước, the commentators said quietly. That's the way to play it when your dream boy tries to talk to you/Yup, you nailed it, and—what's this?—look, she's leaving the field/She's throwing in the towel/She's—

"Oh, do shut up," she muttered.

2

Two knocks on her bedroom wall. It was Jess from next door. *Coffee?* Three taps back. *On my way.*

Her father was already at work, so it was only her mother stern-eyeing her as she hit the kitchen.

"Bye, Ma," she said, picking up her packed lunch from the bench.

"Don't be wasting so much time with Jessica," her mother said in Vietnamese. They always spoke Vietnamese at home. Her mother could speak only a small amount of basic English. Survival English. It was a miracle she could speak it at all after a total of twenty weeks of language class more than twenty years ago. Vân Uớc had always offered to teach her more, but her mother waved it away. *Too late, too late.* She was probably right.

She had only ever worked with other Vietnamese women, hung out with them, shopped in their shops on Albert Street… she didn't need much English to get by. Especially not with a daughter on tap as interpreter/translator.

"Quick coffee, Mama—I'm so early. We get into trouble if we're too early."

Her mother never had a clue about what school approved or disapproved of. That world was as remote and mysterious to her as the moon. She had a generalized fear of the school: it gave her daughter a scholarship; it could take the scholarship away. Vân Ước always had the trump card: all communication from the school was via her. Sometimes it felt mean, and too easy, to play it like this, but it was, finally, an upside of being the family English speaker, whether or not she wanted to be, for all these years.

She chose a banana from the fruit bowl and kissed her mother good-bye.

Her mother nodded and shooed her out dismissively. "Be good. Study hard."

How much did she hate it when her mother said *study hard*? How many times did she have to hear it? (Three thousand six hundred times, she had estimated. Give or take.)

She walked to Jess's, the twelve big steps along the concrete hallway that used to be sixteen steps when they were little. The metal screen door was open, the coffee ready. Jess's parents, both cleaners at the local public hospital, were working early shifts and long gone.

"Your mum would kill you," Vân Ước said, nodding at the open door.

Jess shrugged. "She's not happy unless I'm giving her something to kill me about." She handed over the coffee in a tall glass. "How was IB day one?"

Vân Ước took a sip. Instant, mixed with a heap of condensed milk and some boiling water. A Vietnamese specialty. A great heart starter for the walk to school. It made you fly on a little cloud of sugar and caffeine. One of the many off-curriculum things she had learned at Crowthorne Grammar was that instant coffee was a crime, a hideous faux pas. If you didn't pay four bucks and have someone else make it for you, it wasn't coffee. They didn't know what they were missing.

"Eck—the usual. More work than I signed up for," she said, thinking, IB had started weirdly. With Billy Gardiner *talking to me* after school. She wouldn't tell Jess about that until she'd figured it out. "How's year eleven going?"

"Same. All they've done basically is tell us it's more work than we realize and we'd better work like we mean it from day one if we want to compete blah-dy blah..."

Jess's school—Vân Ước's old school—offered the standard year eleven and year twelve Victorian Certificate of Education program. Crowthorne Grammar offered VCE plus an alternative, encouraged for the smarter students: the IB program. It was crazy that Vân Ước had won a scholarship to Crowthorne Grammar in year nine and Jess hadn't. Their scores all through school had been pretty much on par. They switched first and second place in most of their subjects. The irony was that Vân Ước—she realized later—got the scholarship because she was so sure she wouldn't. Because of that sudden conviction, she had spoken freely in her interview about what she thought of the current state of politics and society, and her intention to study art eventually, and what her plans were for her art portfolio over the next few years.

Jess had given the more standard, well-behaved answers that they'd been trained to give at scholarship coaching, and she didn't get one. A scholarship. She wasn't lying when she said she was happier to stay where she was at Collingwood Girls Secondary College. And Vân Ước half wished she were still there, too. But the awful truth was that Vân Ước had made her parents happy and proud, and Jess had disappointed hers and caused them to lose money when the coaching didn't pay off. The old joke was that the Asian "fail" was an A-, but in truth the Asian fail was not getting a scholarship. Vân Ước also had what the girls called the "oboe advantage," playing one of the more obscure instruments for orchestra. It had only been chosen for her because her father had found the instrument sleeping in its crimson-lined case in a pawn shop on Bridge Road for twenty dollars. Jess was just one more violinist.

• • •

Along Albert Street the shops were opening, and footpaths being washed clean of late-night vomit and early-morning dog pee. It was Thursday, so all the restaurants with toilets out the back would already have locked those doors. Government benefits payment day was also look-for-a-handy-place-to-hit-up day.

"Vân Ước, Jessicaaa!" The girls stopped at the doorway from which the screaming had come. It was Liên Luu from their block. She managed a bakery, the sort that had an improbably large selection of sweet and savory bread products, and—lucky day—she had a couple of misshapen fruit buns to give away. Liên Luu was also the auntie of cool Henry Ha Minh, of Henry Ha Minh Rolls fame.

The two girls walked and talked and chewed their way past the security-grilled, graffitied, and bilingually signed tailors, dry cleaners, two-dollar shops where most of the stuff cost more like five dollars, fishmongers, kitchen-supply places, huge grocers and electrical goods stores, and many "original" *phở* joints so beloved of Melbourne's middle class.

Now, of course, second-generation Vietnamese kids had their upmarket witty designer versions of all this food at three times the price and away from the mini Saigons of Richmond and Footscray and Box Hill. Henry was one of them. Henry Ha Minh Rolls was on Chapel Street and always had a queue of people waiting outside. Vân Ước and Jess worked there on Saturdays making rice paper rolls or, if they were on the early shift, doing prep for making rice paper rolls.

The girls gave each other their standard two-way bro-knuckle farewell and went in opposite directions when they hit Punt Road.

3

Lou stopped Vân Ước, wandering out to lunch after a morning of physics. Vân Ước had been hoping to bump into Lou or Michael, who, while not exactly friends, were certainly friend*ly* toward her. They would never ignore her if she sat down in their vicinity at lunchtime.

"Are you coming to the thing?" Lou was reading from a handout. "The 'How Can I Contribute to the Community?' briefing?"

"I forgot." *Great. More work.* This was a part of CAS— Creativity, Action, Service. It was a compulsory part of IB and sought to ensure all students were also fully rounded human beings. How much spare time did the IB curriculum developers think students had? They were kidding if they thought human, let alone humane, had a chance; there was barely enough time to be efficient study-bots.

• • •

Lou had only come to Crowthorne Grammar in fourth term last year, a new girl for the Mount Fairweather outdoor education program, a boarding semester, located away from the city campus. In the space of one term, Lou had put herself into a position of strength in the pack, without seeming to try or to care. She had her own rung—or maybe she had her own ladder. She stood up for weaker animals. She had a moral platform. She had a super-high-kudos skill—singing. And she had some extra cachet thanks to having lesbian mothers. Which seemed to have been judged as cool.

When Vân Ước had told her about Lou, Jess actually whooped and air-punched at the lesbian-mother revelation, an unusual display of enthusiasm. Jess was a lesbian—or, as she preferred to describe herself, a lesbian-in-waiting.

She'd known she wasn't straight since forever but believed to the tips of her toenails that there was no way she could come out to her parents until she left school and could support herself, because it was more likely they would get the locks changed than accept her sexuality. She was philosophical about it, seeing it for now as a generalized no-go zone rather than a cop-out, because she knew her parents would object to any brand of romantic attachment while she was at school.

The only thing Jess could imagine changing her parents'

view of the desirability of having a lesbian daughter was if Penny Wong (a hero to both the girls) one day became prime minister of Australia. Lesbian Asian prime minister might just tip the balance in Jess's favor. But then again...

• • •

"We can take our lunch in," Lou said. "They're getting us used to doing at least two things at once at all times for the next two years. Cheers, guys."

About half of year eleven was settling in the main assembly hall, with high-volume chat and rustle. This vast space of high ceilings and long windows and good acoustics and a professional-grade stage also had a parquetry floor so smooth and deeply glossy that Vân Ước had promised herself a sock-skate alone in here one day before she left school next year.

She sat with Lou and Michael. On her other side was Annie, someone who lived in such a state of perpetual motion that sitting next to her meant shrinking inside the boundaries of your own space for fear of elbows, feet, and pen jabs, while Annie reliably exceeded her own allocation of space.

As Ms. King, who coordinated CAS and was also overall year-eleven coordinator, settled everyone down and started explaining the service component of CAS—eliciting groans as she laid down the law about needing to organize your volunteer schedule *yesterday*—Vân Ước was aware of greater-than-usual wriggle activity from Annie's direction. As she turned to ask Annie to stop bumping her, she found herself face-to-face with Billy Gardiner, who'd apparently swapped seats with Annie. He gave Vân Ước a satisfied smile and leaned in to look at her lunch.

"Yum," he said, helping himself to one of her mother's little stuffed omelets, a first-week-back treat. "Delicious!" he said, mouth full. "Did you make these?" He looked at the spilling coriander and chicken and bean sprouts as though the omelet were the subject of an intense forensic investigation. "What's in here?"

Vân Ước felt her cheeks burn with embarrassment. She had not sat down expecting to be the subject of one of Billy Gardiner's mean jokes. Was he about to spit the food out and pretend to be sick? She felt sick herself at what might be coming next. She covered up the rest of her lunch.

Lou, seeing what was happening, leaned forward, speaking into Vân Ước's silence. "Quit stealing food!"

"Not stealing, swapping," Billy said, opening a grocery-size paper bag. "What would you like?"

He put the bag on Vân Ước's lap and rummaged about, pulling out a container of strawberries that he waved under her nose. She shook her head, eyes forward, dreading the inevitable punch line, where she'd become the butt of his joke, or perhaps the recipient of a nasty nickname. What had she done to deserve his attention? He was elbowing her now. "How about...a homemade muesli bar?" She shook her head again, determined not to look at him. More rummaging. "Orange cake?" Vân Ước squirmed sideways, closer to Lou, pushing Billy's lunch bag from her lap. "Okay, you got it—chicken schnitzel and coleslaw focaccia...halves?" He produced a massive slab of a sandwich and offered it to Vân Ước. She turned away. "I mean, there must be something here you like. An apple? What sort of food *do* you like?"

"Leave her alone, Gardiner," said Michael from two seats away.

"I'm just trying to share," Billy said.

"Tune in, please, year elevens," Ms. King was saying.

Billy leaned in so he was almost touching Vân Ước's face. She braced herself. Here it came, the punch line. "You know her name's Jo, right?" Billy was nodding to the front of the room. His blue eyes shone with the silliness of the revelation—that miraculously had nothing to do with her. "Joanne. Jo King. True story."

She risked meeting his glance for a second. Nothing but his wide, mischievous smile, directed at her with no apparent malice. This made no sense. Billy Gardiner did not initiate conversation or crack jokes with the Vân Ước Phans of the world.

"What about your name, Vân Ước—what does that mean? What's the translation?"

"Cloudwish."

"Cloudwish? *Cloudwish.* That's so cool. And unusual. Is it, like, a family name, or what?"

He was waiting for a response. He had to be taking the piss. Didn't he realize most names meant something? His name, William, for instance, meant "helmet." Tragic that she'd looked it up. She gave herself a mental shake and looked around for one or more of his friends laughing on the sidelines. The dare, the bet, won. Pretend like you're friends with the povvo Asian chick.

She tuned back in to Ms. King without giving him an answer.

"Now, for anyone without work lined up, can we have some brainstorming—some networking—hands up—sharing some ideas, please, for where we might look for work."

A couple of reluctant hands went up.

"Visiting old people."

"Children's hospital."

Annie's hand shot up. "Refugees!" she said, obviously relieved to have thought of something. She leaned across Billy to Vân Ước, looking mortified. "OMIGOD, I'm so sorry, I didn't mean *you*."

Billy bristled. "Vân Ước's not a refugee, you retard; she's Australian."

Lou bristled. "Can you *not* use ableist language, Billy?"

Annie bristled. "I said I didn't *mean* her."

Vân Ước bristled. "There's nothing *wrong* with being a refugee."

They were all confused. The roles were muddied. What on earth, Vân Ước wondered, was she doing speaking out like that? She, the silent one. Sounding so bossy. And what was Billy Gardiner doing defending her?

"Billy, Vân Ước, Lou, Annie—you can stay and pack up chairs when we finish, thanks," said Ms. King.

● ● ●

"Great. This is the thanks I get for thinking of the refugees," said Annie, slamming another chair onto the pile and looking at Vân Ước. "*Sorry*. Again. It's just I wouldn't mind having ten minutes of my lunchtime. Have you guys got your volunteer stuff organized?"

"A couple of maybes, but nothing interesting," said Lou.

Billy picked up four chairs as though they were feathers. "Me neither. Only thing on offer is crunching data on my father's research project. Which I'd rather blow off my own balls than do." Billy's father was a high-profile doctor involved in developing new treatments for melanomas.

"What I really hate about it is that I know for sure a whole lot of people will fake at least half their hours, and suckers like me will actually be doing the work," said Annie.

"Do you know what you're doing?" asked Lou.

"I'm trying to get onto a coastal revegetation program," said Annie. "Who knew you've got to beg to be allowed to help places?" She crashed another chair onto the pile. "And I'm only marginally eligible for IB, so I'm basically screwed from day one." Annie had just scraped into the program, but her parents had promised the school she'd lift her game academically if they let her in.

"What about you, Vân Ước?" asked Lou.

"I'm working at a tutor program for kids whose parents have English as a second language."

"Oh, I'd love to do that—do they need anyone else?"

Vân Ước hesitated. Someone like Lou would be fantastic to have at homework club, but if she encouraged her to come along, she'd be breaking one of her golden rules: keep school life and home life separate.

"It's pretty grotty. Very noisy. Mostly kids from the East

Melbourne public housing apartments." Kids like her, actually. It was thanks in part to her weekly sessions with her tutor, Debi, that Vân Ước was as well-read, with as good an English vocab, as anyone else in her class.

"When is it?" asked Billy.

"Fridays at five o'clock."

"And what's the deal?"

How to describe the heaving bustle that somehow sorted itself into shape every week? "About two hundred kids and about two hundred tutors meet at the St. Joey's church hall and sit around tables, and for an hour the tutors help the kids with their homework. Or schoolwork in general. Or life in general. Sometimes the mothers come and get help, too. All the kids get a snack and a juice box. The ones who need a lift get bused back to the apartments that are farther away."

"Sounds excellent," Billy said. "And it's my only training-free afternoon—I can do it, too."

"Yeah, only you weren't invited yet," said Lou, rolling her eyes at Vân Ước. "Despite being an entitled white male, you do still need the occasional invitation."

"I can come, can't I?" Billy looked at Vân Ước beseechingly. "Please let me."

Vân Ước, Lou, and Annie looked at him. What was going on with that?

"I'll ask," said Vân Ước reluctantly. "You can't just show up, though. You need to get a Working with Children check."

"Okay, well, let me know, Vân Ước," said Lou. "I'd love to do it if they need someone. I'm happy to tutor any subject, any age group."

"Me too," said Billy.

She was so used to Billy Gardiner mocking, joking, and generally doing anything to get a laugh that it was difficult to believe he was being serious.

4

Vân Ước headed home down the Punt Road hill, along the river toward Church Street, and across the bridge, stopping halfway to peer into the murky Yarra waters and up over the city skyline. Instead of listening to French dialogue exercises on her iPod, she spent the whole time trying to work out the Billy Gardiner puzzle.

Her first assumption was the only logical conclusion—he must have some well-planned torment in mind for her. No payoff today. He was holding back. Her skin crawled uncomfortably. She stopped, shifted the weight of her bag into a more comfortable position on her back, and pushed her bangs sideways. An elaborate high-stakes bet to try to convince her that he liked her—with a publicly humiliating punch line on the horizon? Like the prom-night-pickup, egg-throwing flashback scene in *Never Been Kissed*. That looked like it really hurt. The best thing she could do was avoid him. She was nothing if not practiced at keeping a low profile.

She examined one of the small proofs that Billy Gardiner had a (well-hidden) heart. Last term at Mount Fairweather, she'd accidentally overheard him speaking to his sister. She knew it was his sister because he'd said *sister call* to Ben Capaldi later in the day when Ben asked. Every phone call at Mount Fairweather was newsworthy, because they were so strictly limited.

Vân Ước had been cleaning and packing up her oboe, and he must have been leaning against the wall right outside the practice room, speaking on the school office phone, which you weren't supposed to take out of the office. Rules and Billy! She was too shy to open the door and walk out past him, so she stayed put. His sister had obviously broken up with a boy-friend. And Billy was…perfect. He was supportive and affectionate. He listened. He acknowledged her feelings but was confident she'd feel better before too long. He reminded her of the importance of eating chocolate and watching some *Gilmore Girls* and *Veronica Mars*. And he ended the call by saying, *I always knew the guy was a douche*, which, she could tell, made his sister laugh, because he started laughing, too, and said, *That's more like it*. And he said, *Call me again anytime*. And he said, *I love you, okay?*

She trudged along Albert Street. It also had to be said that Billy Gardiner was smart. The kind of smart that bugged teachers. He appeared to be paying no attention but then could answer questions designed to catch him out. He seemed to divide his concentration with no apparent effort.

The heat of the asphalt footpath burned through the soles of her shoes. Occasional delicious wafts of coriander and garlic and lemongrass floated from restaurant doors. She weaved her well-known course, giving the junkies a wide berth, her private-school uniform being a got-some-spare-change-love magnet, and saw someone she knew at least every few blocks all the way home.

Walking onto the grounds of the apartments, she admired the familiar long shadow her building cast into the end of the hot afternoon.

Great. Nick Sparrow and his friends were on the playground. Most little kids were already inside for dinnertime. And the ones who weren't buzzed off anyway when the big boys came into their space.

"Chick-ay—chickee, chickee. Chick-ay! Lady want some D?" Nick grabbed his crotch and gyrated his hips.

Really? She really had to listen to Nick Sparrow doing a B-grade street thug impersonation from some American crime show? In broad daylight—on her own turf? She looked to see exactly who was with him. Matthew Trần and three other boys she knew from West Abbotsford Primary School. Normally she would have treated them as invisible and walked on. Was it that she was finally in year eleven, the end of school and the beginning of life in sight? Or that she was discombobulated by the bizarre Billy Gardiner treatment? She did not lower her eyes and walk on. She would not let them make her feel uncomfortable. She willed herself to say something. Say anything—now. Right now would be a good time. Put these dummies in their place.

Nothing came out.

She turned as crisply as she could on the tanbark and walked off, hoping she at least looked as angry as she felt. Even if she hadn't managed to open her mouth. What had stopped her from saying something? As she walked into the building's lobby, she felt that she'd let the whole team down: herself, *Jane Eyre*, and Debi.

• • •

The overlocker was thumping away in her parents' bedroom. Her mother did three or four days a week of piecework sewing these days, which was like semiretirement compared to when Vân Ước was little. It was baby onesies again, she could tell by the pale blue fabric fiber on the kitchen bench where her mum had unpacked and counted the precut garments. Vân Ước grabbed an apple and headed into her room for a couple of hours of homework before dinner.

She and her tutor, Debi, had read *Jane Eyre* at homework club, starting at the beginning of year eight. It felt way too hard at first. The vocab! She still had her lists. *Cavillers, moreen, lamentable, letter-press, promontories, accumulation, realms, vignettes, eventide, torpid, hearth, crimped, stout, dingy, lineaments, visage, gorged, bilious, bleared, sweetmeats, morsel, menaces, inflictions, mused, tottered, equilibrium, rummage, tyrant, pungent, predomi-nated, subjoined*... and that was just the first chapter. The feeling of panic, of ignorance, of despair at ever mastering this truck-load of indigestible words! They were not words she heard at home. She was the only one in the family who was ever going to read books like *Jane Eyre*.

Debi's face lighting up as Vân Ước read the first line—*There was no possibility of taking a walk that day*—was still a vivid memory. Nothing was as contagious as Debi's enthusiasm for reading.

"I am a complete nut for this book," Debi had said. "My year-eight teacher made us write a chapter-by-chapter summary, and it was a good thing. It made me feel that I owned the book. I knew it inside out."

Vân Ước decided that she, too, would get to know the book inside out. And something miraculous happened when they were about a quarter of the way through reading it. After weeks of plowing and hesitating, something clicked; she stopped stumbling over the unknown words and long sen-tences. Words magically started to reveal meaning, most of the time anyway, through context. And the sentences themselves stopped being obstacles and started telling a story. Her eyes were racing ahead; she was comprehending the shape and the rhythm of the language. She was cheering Jane on, and dying to know what would happen next. She suffered all Jane's indig-nities and humiliations and, in the end, triumphed with her.

She and Debi talked about each passage after she read it aloud, and discussed the era in which it was written, the restrictions and expectations imposed on a character like Jane, and on all women, in different ways, according to their strata of society; they talked about the importance of religious faith in the era, the way in which people with mental illness were generally treated—and at the end of the book, Debi said, "Never listen to fools who dis *Jane Eyre* as being a story about a girl who gets her mean man. This is a character who gets what she wants and lives on her own terms by having moral fortitude, intelligence, courage, imagination, and a will of iron. And that is one hell of a checklist. Imagine Charlotte Brontë writing this book in 1847. What a powerful story for women living at that time!"

Vân Ước agreed. Poor Charlotte Brontë had had to use a dude name to get the book published at first: Currer Bell. That was how undervalued women were.

Vân Ước got into the habit of calling Jane to mind pretty much whenever courage was required or justice denied. She privately used the test: *What would Jane do?* As if Jane were hanging around the apartments. Or trying to fit in imperceptibly—a poor kid at a rich school. She often thought about exactly what Jane would say or do, what she herself should have said or done in various situations. She remembered Nick Sparrow, with a hot flare of annoyance. One day she'd find the guts to say what Jane would in a situation like that.

Out loud.

Note to self.

Promise to self.

5

Her *ba*, father, had dinner nearly ready by the time she emerged from a trance of non-Euclidean geometry. It was one of his special dishes, fish with pink peppercorns, ginger, and coriander. When he cooked this dish, he always said the same thing, "Some people pay for this pepper in the fancy shops. But not us."

"Not us," Vân Ước repeated.

"No, we go to the riverbank," he said. "Because *we* know—"

"We know where the peppercorns grow." She smiled, wondering how many times they'd had this exchange since she was little.

Her father's grandparents had been market gardeners, and of her parents he was the one who preferred cooking. On any of their walks, he always had his eye out for food that could be foraged: onion weed, milk thistle, amaranth, and wild rocket along the railway line; lemons and plums hanging over alley-way fences; the peppercorn tree on the river bend five minutes' walk from where they lived. He had planted *rau răm*, Vietnam-ese mint, near the peppercorn tree, and that now grew there in plentiful supply. They nursed along the more temperamental coriander in pots on the kitchen windowsill.

By eleven thirty, her parents had been asleep for nearly two hours, she'd snuck quietly into the kitchen to make a late-night icy Milo (an addiction she'd brought home from Mount Fairweather), and all her homework was finished, except for a polish on the creative writing piece.

She stirred her drink, smelling the cold malty goodness, let-ting the ice cubes clink into the side of the glass, staring into the fractured reflection in the window over her desk.

Because all her common sense told her that Billy Gardiner was likely—veering to certainly—going to act according to the character she had observed for the last two years and that it was likely-veering-to-certain that he had something mean planned for her, it hit her like a heart attack when she remem-bered the wish. The ridiculous, frivolous, throwaway wish...

Because...because his strange behavior since that class yesterday—that she had interpreted—*was interpreting*—as preparatory to some sort of mean joke—could also be inter-preted as (gulp) Billy liking her because she had wished that he would. She breathed in some Milo instead of swallowing and almost choked. What words had she used as she made the wish? That he would *prefer her to all other girls*, find her *fascinating*? No. No way. It was embarrassing to even let herself entertain the idea for one second. And yet, how else to explain his apparent vehemence on her behalf as he said, *she's Australian*...? Annoying, of course, because was it such an automatic virtue to be "Australian"—though his intention was to elevate her from "refugee," another annoyance, because of the automatic low-status assumption that always came with that label—but that aside...

She didn't believe in fairies, zombies, vampires, Father Christmas—or magic wishes. That stuff was for kids. She drank some more Milo, spooning up the cold crunchy bits from the top. She looked inside her pencil case for the umpteenth time. Surely the little glass vial couldn't have just disappeared. She ran a finger around the inside seam, under the zipper, and tipped everything out onto her desk. Still not there.

Wishes were not a thing.

They were not.

Correction.

Wishes *were* a thing.

Wishes that came true were sometimes a thing.

Wishes that came true *because of magic* were not a thing.

• • •

To pull her mind back into shape, she decided to give herself some free writing; after the refugee conversation today, a little vent on what not to say to Asian kids...and some retorts she wished she could occasionally deliver, rather than just think.

Where are you from?

Australia, fool, same as you.

Where are you really from?

Are you still here? My parents were both born in Vietnam, but they are also Australian citizens.

Wow, that food looks so interesting and unusual; you're so lucky.

It's just what we eat at my place. Try to peep over that giant Western outlook. A sandwich is not the default lunch for the entire world.

You're a "hot Asian." You're an "Asian nerd."

You do realize those are dehumanizing racist stereotypes, not compliments? No? Well, now you know.

Do you have a Tiger Mother?

Sometimes my mother is a tiger; sometimes she's a moth, fragile and vulnerable.

Do you get into trouble if you don't get straight As?

It's never happened, but if it did, I could lose my scholarship. I don't have a safety net like you do.

Do you get sunburned?

Yes, and I also bleed. I even go to the bathroom. Just like a real human. Who knew!

How much for the Asian schoolgirl double act?

Do you realize we are actual schoolgirls, old-loser-guys-calling-out-from-cars? Probably pretty much the same age as your own daughters. We are not on an excursion from a brothel.

Are you going to do law, or medicine?

Neither. (But don't tell my parents.)

Do your parents own a restaurant?

My mother does piecework from home, and my dad works in a food-processing factory cutting up chickens into portions.

You look like Lucy Liu.

An actor who is old enough to be my mother? Because we both have long black hair? Or because all Asians look alike? (I don't.) (And we don't.)

Select All. Delete.

Swallowing a laugh, she imagined printing it out and distributing it.

It felt brilliant to bash things out in black and white.

Thank you, Ms. Bartloch.

6

Walking to school, early on Friday morning, Vân Ước decided that she was in-waiting every bit as much as Jess was. She wasn't at all interested in any of the boys she knew from primary school. And Billy Gardiner would never be interested in her, despite his recent aberrant behavior.

If she had to be in unrequited love with someone, which seemed annoyingly to be the case, surely logic should have pointed her in the direction of Michael. Kind, brainy, handsome, and his own endearing brand of very odd. Because he himself was in unrequited love with Sibylla Quinn, Michael would be a perfect unavailable person with whom to be in unrequited love.

It was mystifying and annoying being attracted to Billy.

Just yesterday he christened their perfectly nice physics teacher, Mr. Hodge, "Pigman" Pigman Podge. True, he did have a piggy nose and some unfortunate food spillage on his button-down vest front, but really...

Billy had even once said, unbelievably, that sylphlike Sibylla Quinn danced like a *spastic tarantula*. No doubt about it, he had a nasty streak. He got away with plenty because he made people laugh. But he had his enemies. And he could be a bully. He seemed to despise weak people. That meant he was probably afraid of whatever his own well-hidden weaknesses were. Billy's best friend was Ben Capaldi, who strategically sought to stay on everyone's good side but hid it so well that no one seemed to notice.

But nature clearly didn't understand logic. When she thought about Billy, she was selective. She let the meanness shrink and the kindness grow. She considered the balance and symmetry and physical ease he so effortlessly embodied, the strong twist of desire that tightened within her whenever they accidentally stood close together, the hard beauty of his face, which always called to her mind the words *fallen angel*.

And, irresistibly appealing though this was, nothing was quite as intriguing as the thing he was hiding. She might be the only one who stood quietly enough, looked closely enough, to see it. Flickering almost imperceptibly around the edges of him was a restlessness, or dissatisfaction. It reminded her of the moment just before the Incredible Hulk started hulking.

● ● ●

She entered the school grounds through a side gate, and as she skirted the back of the gym building, she was startled by a large, sweaty boy throwing himself through the doorway, bending over and vomiting violently. It was Billy Gardiner, clad only in bike shorts. He straightened up, panting, spitting, and groaning in pain.

She looked the other way, earbuds in, and kept walking.

Billy called her name; she pretended not to hear him.

He must have been doing ergos. Places in the first eight rowing crew were constantly assessed. One expectation was that the rowers would exert themselves to the utmost in the regular training tests on the ergometers, the fixed rowing machines. Only the fittest, with exactly the right body type— long, strong, lean—could even think about signing up for the privilege of this much discomfort and pain. And then having to prove over and over again their fitness and commitment. On the river at ungodly hours for much of the year. In a cycle of competition with the other private schools that had become bizarrely fierce, and saw the training season lengthen to the point where all the rowers were risking their backs with the sheer brutal repetition the sport now required.

Despite this, a line of contenders shadowed the girls' and

the boys' first crews, nanoseconds off the pace, all putting their hands up for places in the top crews.

Vân Ước had zero competitive spirit when it came to sports. But among the elite rowers, it was intense; there was a belief that if you didn't vomit after your ergo, you hadn't really tried. That seemed all kinds of weird to her. What did it really matter if your crew rowed one fraction of a second faster or slower than another school's crew? Deep in speculation of this imponderable, alien behavior of her adopted tribe here at Crowthorne Grammar, she nearly jumped out of her shoes when Billy clapped his hand on her shoulder to get her attention.

"Sorry." He registered her startle with an apologetic grimace.

"That's okay." Vân Ước readjusted her book-heavy backpack.

Seeing her uncomfortable shrug seemed to prompt Billy. He took the pack off her back in a swift, unexpected move and started walking along beside her, still bare-chested, carrying it.

She could see him chucking it over a fence, dumping it in the boys' bathroom, or opening it and emptying its contents across the oval they were crossing. "Can I please…?" She reached over to take it back.

"This weighs a ton." Billy looked at his watch. "Shit. I still have to shower—we'll talk later."

Vân Ước was still holding out a hand for her pack, trying not to show the panic brimming up inside her.

"I'll drop it at your locker." He took off at a run across the oval, her bag on his back.

What the hell was he doing? Her laptop was in there. Her

lunch. Her jumper. All her English and math books. Her precious camera, as good as new from Cash Converters. The day's supply of tampons. Stuff she couldn't afford to lose. She mightn't be able to keep up with Billy, but she was determined not to lose sight of that bag. She followed him at a sprint. She'd kept up her fitness from Mount Fairweather, still running at least three times a week, and was no more than twenty yards behind by the time he arrived at, thank god, the year eleven and twelve center. And miraculously—yes!—he was heading in the direction of the lockers.

Holly, Tiff, and Ava arrived just in time to see Vân Ước apparently chasing Billy Gardiner, panting after him, into the year-eleven locker area.

"Oh, please, that's just pathetic," said Holly.

"She can run all she likes, but she won't catch him," said Tiff. Ava snorted with derision.

Billy had put Vân Ước's bag down by the time she reached her locker. "Aren't you going to ask how I did in my ergo?"

"How did you do?" Vân Ước and Holly spoke at the same time.

"Aced it," he said, grinning, then turned to run back to the sports center. "Six thirty."

Holly walked up to her, standing too close. "He wasn't talking to *you*." She and Ava burst out laughing at the very thought.

Vân Ước had no illusions about where she sat in the pecking order around here: rock bottom. But one thing, no matter how strange, was clear. Billy had made eye contact with her. He was

41

talking to her, and it was an amazingly good ergo time. She wasn't proud that she'd covertly researched Billy's preferred sports. Some days it was as though her fingers had minds of their own when she opened her browser. She unzipped her backpack—still damp with his sweat—and, as she started unpacking her books in a daze, overheard Ava say to Holly, "Babe, you would so be going out with him if Head of the River wasn't about to happen."

Vân Ước could tell from Holly's elaborately casual, "Oh maybe, I don't know, it's just a couple of friendly hookups," how much she wanted it to be the case.

• • •

It took her most of the day to resettle; already a difficult task given that her first portfolio meeting was scheduled for after last period.

Ms. Halabi, the art teacher, jumped straight in. "Tell me about some work I can't wait to see."

It meant so much to Vân Ước that the idea of not being able to share her vision for her art was terrifying, almost paralyzing. But gradually her racing heart slowed to a normal pace as she talked through some of her concepts and plans for the two years' work and saw her teacher's enthusiasm.

She showed Ms. Halabi a handful of early studies, close-ups. She'd been shooting a secret treasury of small stamped-in pieces of metal that studded the footpaths around where she lived.

How they got there, and whether or not they had some functional purpose, she didn't know. As a little girl, she'd imagined them to be valuable ancient coins working their way up from deep inside the earth: buried treasure. Even now, knowing there were no ancient coins in this land, they still held a magic for her.

Bright beaten pieces of silver, half buried in the blue-black asphalt. Maybe they were surveyors' markers. Sometimes they were encircled by a spray of paint. Stamped over by a thousand footfalls. Trampled. Modest. Unnoticed. She was going to make a piece of art that showed the iridescent beauty of these faux coins. She had chosen twelve and was patiently shooting them at all hours of daylight, as the sun played across their surface. She would make a grid that looked like a piece of shimmering chain mail. Imagining it was just the beginning. She'd have to shoot and compose 144 images to make a single portfolio piece.

She planned to apply the same patterning principle to some other materials. The next piece would be made up of photographs of the old, mottled green and purple glass tiles that still survived unobtrusively on some Melbourne city footpaths. They were skylights to the basement level of the Victorian-era buildings and looked like jewels erupting from the seams of buildings and footpaths.

She'd shoot and compose a similar number of these images. The portfolio would have six pieces in total. She wanted the work to show that the seemingly insignificant could warrant close attention, and the tiniest elements could be made monumental. Indeed, she wanted to invert the whole idea of what was/should be considered monumental.

Seen together, she hoped the pieces in her portfolio would create a picture of the city she knew—vast, but stitched together from tiny pieces and small moments.

She wanted her art to carry such a load of ideas and was terrified that her ambition would outstrip her ability and that the work she produced could never quite glean her teeming brain, to borrow from John Keats.

By the time she'd finished trying to share the vision that was so clear in her mind, she could feel her face burning with concentration.

Ms. Halabi was nodding. "Plenty of nice chewy thematic complexity and technical challenges to keep you busy for the two-year program. I can't wait to see more. I want you to keep in mind that image of these pieces as a suite as you proceed, because this work is also going to drive you truly crazy at least half a dozen times. You'll need to remind yourself how magnificent it will all be once realized."

"I know. It's fiddly."

"I'll leave you with two thoughts: one practical, one theory-based." The art teacher held up one paint-stained finger. "Five minutes spent cleaning a disk with a rag and some methylated spirits might save you two hours of photoshopping." She raised a second finger, also ingrained with paint. "And— consider the meaning of these images. Every time you're working with them, ask yourself: What do they mean? And, even more important, what do they mean *to me*? The more specific and personal something is, the more its universality emerges."

The more specific and personal…

Fine.

Personal and *specific* were not muscles that got a lot of flexing in her family. But she'd try. Another solo flight. It's not like she wasn't used to that.

There probably weren't two words that pushed her harder toward the gaping holes in her life. Gaps and question marks all over the place.

7

Every year, around this time, for as long as Vân Ước could remember, her mother got sick. It was as though she just disappeared, curled up inside her shell like a snail poked with a stick.

She'd realized a couple of years ago that it wasn't as simple as her *ba* made out: her mother was more than just tired. Eventually it clicked that her mother's slump time coincided with the time of year her parents had left Vietnam. They got the diagnosis last year: relapsing post-traumatic stress disorder, PTSD. This year it was getting treated properly. Not just the symptoms, either. This year things would be different. Fingers crossed.

• • •

It's complicated (that Facebook cliché) was in fact the perfect description for her relationship with her parents. It was the same for all the first-generation Vietnamese Australian kids she knew.

The deal with parents who'd survived the sort of horror you didn't even want to know about was that you shared the weight of all the risks they'd taken (for you), all the suffering they'd gone through (so you wouldn't have to suffer), the deprivation they'd signed up for (so you would want for nothing), and all the terrifying dislocation they felt (so you'd have a home, feel at home). It was pretty tough, really. For all concerned.

If only the love and irritation could merge into a calm neutrality, but they didn't. They were like oil and water. Each with a determined integrity. One or the other. No blending. No blanding.

Debi had helped give some context to that pressure to be happy, to be successful. Her mother had been a Holocaust survivor, which was right up there with the worst anyone's parents might have endured.

• • •

This was everything she'd heard directly from her mother about her parents' exodus from Vietnam to Australia:

From when she was little, she'd asked questions. When had her parents moved from Vietnam to Australia? Her father told her they'd left Vietnam by boat, arrived in Malaysia, and been transferred to Australia. She'd stirred that up in her mind with Noah's ark for a few years, but it clarified over time into the less poetic reality.

Her parents were "boat people," though when they arrived in Australia the expression wasn't so venom-coated.

Her mother was twenty-one years old when they left Vietnam in 1980. Her father was one year older. Her auntie, Hoa Nhung, who apparently lived in Sydney but whom they never saw, was on the boat with them. She was nineteen when they left. And why did they never speak to her? Why had she never visited?

Years after their eventual arrival in Darwin (via the mosquito-infested Malaysian island they felt so blessed to have landed on), after relocating to Melbourne (first stop: Lansdowne Hostel), after compulsory but inadequate language classes, after settling for work in their second language that was less than it might have been, after the allocation of public housing, seventeen years after all that, Vân Ước was born.

So her parents were also old, on top of everything else.

Was her name, Vân Ước—Cloudwish—connected to the time no one would speak about?

Why the long wait?

Did her parents have fertility problems?

Did they not want a child?

Did they change their minds?

Was she an accident?

And who were the two little girls in the photo she'd found, snooping through her mother's chest of drawers when she was twelve, and which she took out periodically to reexamine in secret? If it was her mother and Hoa Nhung, why was it hidden away? Why wasn't it out in a frame, like Vân Ước's horrible grade-six graduation photo? Or her even more horrible First Holy Communion photo?

What was the story?

Because of her parents' reticence, it had become unthinkable to broach any of these questions with them. Her *ba* only ever said: *Don't ask your mother about it. It was a hard time. A bad time.*

Vân Ước had eventually stitched together some possibilities—just what she'd gleaned from her own research. She only unfolded that ugly little garment—still full of missing stitches—in private, trying to understand exactly what her parents might have survived.

How was she supposed to feel about it? Proud? Fearful? Ashamed?

When she looked at her parents watching *MasterChef* on TV in a tired trance at the end of the working day, she could not connect the very ordinariness of them to what she'd read.

What they had experienced was obviously unspeakable. But didn't they realize the extent to which not speaking made them strangers to her? Why couldn't they imagine how odd it might feel to see your parents through the wrong end of a telescope?

She thought of demanding that they tell her their story, asking the difficult questions, but her courage always failed. She imagined Jane Eyre, stern-eyed, tapping her polished boot impatiently.

How did their experience fit with her life now? Across this unspoken gulf, where so much was implied but never spelled out, was it really all up to her to justify the effort, the sacrifices? To make it worthwhile? How could she ever do enough, achieve enough? Be enough? To compensate for—what, exactly?

So the boat story morphed from abstract fairy tale to abstract horror as her understanding grew over the years.

She imagined an even more protracted horror story had come before the boat journey: a war, and the aftermath, living under the Communist Party regime following the fall of Saigon. And she was grateful she hadn't thought to find out about that till years later.

She had read about it all now. Like the irresistible pain of wriggling your own loose tooth, she'd found it impossible to stop searching once she started. Every time she found something newly frightening, she challenged herself, with an adrenaline rush, to read it. Many accounts of that time reported grotesque brutality. Her parents were barely out of their teens when they fled. How had they coped with losing everything, with uncertainty, fear, violence?

How would she have coped?

Not well.

But would she have had the ingenuity and the guts to escape?

Not likely.

So, frustrating though her gentle parents were, demanding

though they were, dependent though they were, they were also her heroes, her superiors in every sense, and she would rather die than disappoint them. Even if it killed her.

Gaps and question marks were only part of the problem.

How was she ever going to convince her parents that having an artist for a daughter would not be a complete disaster? At least she wouldn't have to face that conversation till next year. What a wimp. She could virtually hear Jane tsk-tsking in annoyance.

8

After a telephone conversation with her mother's doctor, confirming her antidepressant dosage—from a quick check of the pill package that morning it looked as if she'd stopped taking the medication—Vân Ước was running a few minutes late for homework club.

She arrived as the last students were hurrying in. Vân Ước picked up a grizzly baby, Iman, from her mother, who was sitting with a tutor going through a pile of forms from an insurance company. Iman, happy to be mobile, started flicking the end of Vân Ước's braid back and forth across her own nose, one of her preferred games.

"Did the drink delivery arrive yet?" Aatifa, one of the helper mothers, asked her.

"Yeah—it should be in the back fridge," said Vân Ước. Aatifa took off to start organizing the afternoon snacks they handed around in the last ten minutes of class, and Vân Ước made for a table where she could see a group of tutors with no students allocated to them. She paired the boys up with students, and headed over to the primary school area, of which she was notionally in charge. Everyone was settled and occupied except for one tutor who was trying to deal with a mother who'd walked in hoping to leave her three children that afternoon.

Vân Ước explained to the mother that the kids couldn't stay for today's session, but would have to enroll, and gave the mother some forms to take away, first going through them to make sure she understood everything. She did a lap of the early secondary tables and handed out some extra stationery.

She greeted people, answered questions, made sure that Matthew, the least obnoxious of the guys from her old primary school, was paired with Thy Ngô, now in year eight, who had spoken to her with such excitement about math last year, and as she walked the familiar rounds she tried to imagine what Lou and Billy would make of it.

By halfway through the hour, the volume had increased from a buzz to a roar. It was a hot February day and gusts of air that came in just stirred up the heat and added some grit to the mix. Faces were sheeny with sweat, and a generalized end-of-summer's-day waft of body odor and deodorant wrestled it out with the church hall's own smell, also strong on a hot day, an amalgam of cedar, biscuits, books, and dust.

She could see where Eleanor, who ran the show, was, based on the knot of people surrounding her. Parents trying to ask about everything from scholarships to legal problems, a few shell-shocked-looking teachers who'd brought student tutors along for their first sessions, some little kids who just liked being near Eleanor's knees, and a few regular volunteers who had first-session-back questions.

Vân Ước remembered her first time here as a student, a super-shy fifth grader. Eleanor had introduced her to Debi, saying, *Now, you two, you're going to get along like a house on fire.* That had alarmed Vân Ước, but she took her cue from Debi, who smiled calmly and said, *So, what are you reading, Vân Ước?* And at the end of the session, she'd said to Vân Ước, *You are a terrific reader. See these big girls, here?* Vân Ước had looked around at the older girls who were tutoring students at surrounding tables. *That's going to be you one day. You'll be helping the little ones.* Vân Ước couldn't believe it, but she was proud to be called a strong reader. And it had made her parents happy when she reported the comment to them that night.

Thinking of her parents brought her back to the doctor conversation. No matter how many times she went through it with her mother, the concept of medication taking a while to work never really sank in. Her parents both expected to take a pill and feel the benefits *now*. The medication the doctor had prescribed for her mother called for perseverance and some dosage adjustments. Her mother had started feeling better but was ready to throw in the towel after a week of feeling less well again. Now there'd be another conversation going over everything again. She sighed deeply.

Iman, still on her hip, sighed deeply, too.

Vân Ước had to laugh.

9

On Saturday morning Vân Ước woke with a niggle. Groan. Monday was casual clothes day, which definitely warranted an after-breakfast, before-homework free writing whinge. Topic: money, and lack thereof.

Well, clothes. The embarrassment of looking wrong on casual clothes day. Always a headache.

My school uniform has always been bought secondhand. I have worn every uniform garment I've ever had through the cycle of too big, fits, too small.

Even though I'm a member of orchestra, I'm careful to be the second-best oboist, not the best; my parents won't ever be able to afford the orchestra trip to Europe.

I can't afford coffee after school, except occasionally. I can't afford taxis home after parties. I can't afford the sort of clothes and shoes people wear to parties. I can't afford the presents or alcohol people bring to parties.

Schoolbook lists are a big headache every year. Money is put aside in advance, but it's never enough to stop my parents looking worried. Lots of time trying to find secondhand books. The looming terror of big-ticket items like the laptop, the graphing calculator.

Feet that grow are a big headache.

Conversation about holidays is awkward. I've never been on an official holiday. It's like my parents don't know about the holiday concept. Never even been on an airplane.

I dread being asked, "What did you do over the holidays?"

Special gear for any camp is its own nightmare. The stress of the Mount Fairweather equipment list ruined my life for about six months. What even were some of these things? Gaiters? Headlamp? What could safely be got secondhand? Did I really need the number of multiple items listed? (Yes.) Would my existing knickers and PJs stand public scrutiny? (No.)

I never want to be asked to anyone's house, because I don't want to ask them back here. My parents wouldn't understand or allow that kind of socializing, and I can't even imagine the weird someone might feel when they check out the gap between their natural habitat and mine.

The money from part-time work pays for my (unsmart) phone, public transport, all photography/camera costs not covered by school, all nonuniform clothes and stuff like pool visits and occasional movies during summer holidays.

I don't sign up for any activities that involve parents and transport. I hear about carloads of people getting carted around to debating and weekend sports, but it's never going to include me.

I don't have birthday parties. I don't get invited to birthday parties. I don't mention my birthday in general. I've never had my locker decorated on my birthday at Crowthorne Grammar.

I can't even hang out at the tram stop because walking is cheaper than tramming. Just as well I like walking.

MECCA or MAC free makeovers are only free if you buy some makeup, so that only seems "free" to someone with spare money, i.e., someone who doesn't need a free makeover.

Select All. Delete.

10

Casual clothes day was a gold-coin fund-raiser for year eleven's sponsored student in Somalia. The Somali kid was a distant theory to most of Vân Ước's classmates. It was a safe bet that Vân Ước would be the only person who knew actual Somali kids.

She always gave a two-dollar coin, worried that one dollar might look cheapskate. Lots of kids came with a handful of gold coins, whatever had happened to be in parental purses or pockets that morning, she guessed. And, conversely, people with plenty of money never worried if they didn't have any. Someone like Pippa would be perfectly happy to wander in without a coin, and say, *Who's got a gold coin for little old me?*

She and Jess had workshopped the outfit over the weekend.

Casual clothes day was a competitive fashion parade, for girls anyway, no matter what anyone said or pretended to believe. Vân Ước didn't expect to look good; she just didn't want to look too conspicuously wrong. Jeans. Safe choice. Good label, good fit, thank you, Savers. Converse One Stars. Okay. Not ideal. Good color—crimson. Made unique by hand-drawn curlicues and leaf pattern. Never worn at school before. Burnt orange silk top. Savers. A designer find, nabbed before the vintage store vultures swept through for the armfuls they could mark up by a couple of hundred percent in little North Fitzroy shops. Gorgeous fabric, cut on the bias, it clung and fell just as it should.

Persuaded by Jess, she had submitted to a small amount of eyeliner, and clear lip gloss with a hint of gold shimmer to it. The only thing that could go wrong was the weather.

Being summer in Melbourne, that was exactly what happened.

By the time she was hurrying through the Botanic Gardens, hair whipped around in every direction, the last trails of the hot night had been sucked up by wind swinging to the south. The temperature dropped by ten degrees in five minutes, and cold black coins of rain were landing on the still-warm paths, releasing the scent of toasted asphalt. The rain quickly settled in. Finally, an upside to not owning strappy Italian sandals. She ran to the nearest shelter, a small gazebo with an onion-dome roof, to wait until the downpour eased. She pulled her school rain jacket from her backpack, shivering. Way to kill what was otherwise, for once, an okay casual clothes day outfit.

But what was this? A furry bundle of something on the slatted seat. She gave it a nudge with the back of her finger. It was soft and wooly. Neither mouse, nor cockroach, nor spider scuttled forth. She leaned forward and gave it a cautious sniff. Eucalyptus. She picked it up and shook it gently. It fell open like a fairy-tale dream of Gaultier: a cardigan with long, skinny sleeves knitted in wavering black-and-white stripes…and—what was happening at the shoulders? As though they'd sprouted, fabric petals emerged from each shoulder, red and orange, like wings grading down the upper arms through the rainbow spectrum of colors and flicking out in delicate tips from the elbows in shades of violet. She'd never seen anything like it.

She looked around through the sheeting rain. Who'd left this precious thing behind? Did she dare to try it on? It would make the day so much easier if she could feel warm and comfortable instead of shivering in her slimy rain jacket. She sniffed it properly now, with the experience of the thrift-shop buyer, paying particular attention to the armpits. Fresh as a flower. Slipping it on, she couldn't help but feel as though it had been made for her. The body was cropped exactly at her hip level, the sleeves tapered down covering her long wrists. The wing-petals gave an extra layer of warmth.

As she stroked her fingers along the underside edges of one wing, admiring the amazing construction, she felt the sharp edge of a cardboard tag. Attached with a ribbon and a small black safety pin, it said WEAR ME on one side. She flipped it and read PASS ME ON. Here was some luck. She didn't have to take it off. It was hers, at least for the day. She left the tag on; she would remove it carefully in better light.

As the rain eased, she hitched her backpack on and took a deep breath.

She had not slipped down a rabbit hole.

Nor had a film crew sprung from the shrubbery to announce that she was the subject of a new reality TV show called *That Boy Who Used to Ignore You Notices You Now* or *Find That Attractive Garment in a Public Place*.

This was just life continuing to be a little bit weird.

She hurried to school, trying to beat the next downpour. By the time she walked through the school gates, she was feeling that she might just look…better than okay.

● ● ●

Because it was casual clothes day, the locker area was buzzier than usual. Lots of surreptitious and not so surreptitious checking out, commenting, admiring, teasing. Holly was leaning on her locker door, looking around, hugely amused. "You can so tell that color blindness is more of a guy thing." Tiff and Pippa, the other queens of teen couture, agreed.

As Vân Ước put her backpack into her locker, she remembered the label. She lifted a wing petal, undid the pin carefully, and removed the label, glancing around to see if anyone, other than Michael, had noticed her doing it. Surely it would look slightly strange to come to school in a garment whose tags you apparently hadn't removed.

Holly was looking her way as Vân Ước zipped the label into her backpack pocket, but it seemed she had Michael in her sights.

"And then there's Michael," Holly said. "Oh, the joy of faded black teamed with faded black."

Holly had been breathtakingly nasty to Michael at Mount Fairweather last term, publicly humiliating him by reading out loud an extremely personal letter he'd written about loving Sibylla Quinn. Vân Ước felt hotly uncomfortable for Michael all over again just remembering the way his face had frozen and turned white as Holly read his private words for a laugh. It was interesting to see how he'd gone from mostly ignoring Holly pre-letter-reading incident to retaliating now when she said something mean. He took out his copy of *Ariel* and his English folder from his locker and, even though he clearly couldn't care less about Holly's assessment, said, "Another episode of breathtaking banality from Holly Broderick."

"Loser," Holly said.

"Another stingingly original riposte from Holly Broderick."

Holly looked at him with loathing, but bit her tongue. She recognized superior brainpower when she saw it.

Michael smiled at Vân Ước.

● ● ●

Billy came loping into class, rain-soaked, making wrecked jeans, a washed-out red T-shirt, and sneakers look entirely desirable. There were half a dozen empty places, but he sat next to Vân Ước. She could feel eyebrows go up all over the room. He gave one of her fabric feather/petals a playful tug, saying, "Hey, cool birdie."

Ms. Norton arrived, shushing them and hoping they were old enough not to be distracted by the sartorial splendor they collectively represented.

Vân Ước tried to concentrate on what Ms. Norton was saying, but she'd seen Holly register Billy's compliment, and that would no doubt mean trouble. And Billy Gardiner was sitting right next to her. She could hear him breathe.

Ms. Norton prefaced their discussion of Sylvia Plath with a briefing on the concept of the IB English oral commentaries— formal assessment sessions with your teacher at which selected texts would be discussed. That sounded okay; one-on-one discussion was pretty much what she'd been used to having with Debi at homework club.

Daily class interaction was much more stressful. She hated it when teachers invited her by name to contribute; it meant that she'd misjudged the minimum acceptable level of participation. Ms. Norton, an old-school, strict, English-accented English teacher, was someone from whom she dreaded negative attention.

"More about the orals as we proceed. First, though, can everyone pair up for a practice session? Please choose a partner with whom you have not worked before. I want objective feedback. No friends who already know each other's opinions."

Billy nudged her gently with his elbow. "I'm with Vân Ước."

She looked at him. She could swear he was as surprised as anyone else to hear those words coming out of his mouth.

"Okay," said Ms. Norton. "No need to call out—just take a minute now and partner up. Make a time *outside class hours* to have your session, and we'll have three pairs reporting next class. And do start visiting the intranet subject page regularly."

Vân Ước was trying not to look at Billy. She obviously didn't want to be his partner, but nor did she want to have an attention-drawing altercation in front of the whole class. Maybe she could trade after class. She saw that Polly, a quiet scholarship semi-ally, was with Michael. Though Michael was surely a semi-friend, so maybe out of contention.

Billy Gardiner was a millstone. An attractive millstone. Strange that only days ago a one-on-one session with him would have seemed like a fine idea, but that was just in theory, not real life, so here she was, freaking out.

Couldn't she at least try to forget that this was a complete reversal of previous behavior, one that possibly came from a *wish*, one that would surely draw Holly's attention like an attack dog to raw meat, and relax and enjoy it? Gulp.

Did Sylvia Plath ever have this sort of problem? Was Ted Hughes suddenly everywhere she went, so she felt like she was tripping over him? Although, hadn't Sylvia pursued him? Wasn't there a famous story about her biting his lip till it bled on an early date at a party? That had always sounded more like a spectacularly incompetent kissing episode than anything else. Or maybe until that level of passion hit you, you didn't know it was going to happen. Although, blood—surely that couldn't be a good idea. Spit-swaps must be bad enough—glandular fever had gone around the early kissing brigade like wildfire. Of course that had never been a problem for Vân Ước.

"Please open your copies of *Ariel* to page twenty, and we will look at 'Tulips,'" said Ms. Norton. "Lou, would you like to read it for the class?"

• • •

Holly was looking Vân Ước up and down at the lockers after class. Vân Ước shivered. She'd seen so many people being shredded and spat out by Holly over the last couple of years, even so-called friends, that Vân Ước consciously avoided any contact with her, but now—thanks, Billy—it looked like it was unavoidable. Holly was whispering something to Gabi, one of her cronies, and both were having a little snigger.

Holly, casually resplendent in a new-season Gorman dress, walked up to Vân Ước and ostentatiously walked around her. She plucked at the cardigan's winglike sleeve and said, "Well, what have we come as today? Did someone think it was a costume party?"

Vân Ước turned away and concentrated on packing up her English books and extracting her French folder. It was always worth ignoring a bully as a first strategy.

"I said, what did you come as?"

"Nothing," Vân Ước said.

"Good, just remember that," said Holly.

Vân Ước looked down, refusing to acknowledge Holly with a look or a word. She saved her spleen till she saw Jess after school.

They set down their afternoon snack on a tray between them on the sofa at Jess's—watermelon, rice crackers, hummus, gummy snakes—took off their shoes, and put their feet up on the coffee table.

"What a bitch," said Jess.

"It's her life's work," said Vân Ước.

"So, what would old Jane have done?" Jess knew Vân Ước's *Jane Eyre* habit, and indulged it. She, too, had read and enjoyed *Jane Eyre*, though not to the same semi-obsessive extent as Vân Ước.

"Ha, Jane would wipe the floor with Holly. She'd use the John Reed put-down; she'd say, *Wicked and cruel... You are like a murderer—you are like a slave-driver—you are like the Roman emperors!*"

Vân Ước had a suitable Jane quote for most occasions.

"And what would Holly say to *that*?"

"She'd say, *What are you on, you loser?* And she'd say, *Stay away from Billy.*"

Uh-oh. She hadn't planned to mention the Billy thing.

"Whoa, back up, sister. Billy? Are you talking Billy Gardiner? Dream boy Billy? *Numero uno* mew? You've stopped your preferred charm offensive of pretending to ignore him completely? Give, give, give."

Mew was their own word for anything good or attractive. It started when they were on a reading mission for intel about sex in year seven and came across a steamy romance in which the sappy heroine, Brandy, *mewed* in a moment of sexual passion. That cracked them up; they cried with laughter. They immediately chose a preferable animal whose spirit they might invoke while having sex—if that ever happened. Jess decided on a walrus, thinking a loud honk might be just the thing to get a laugh in the sack; Vân Ước went for a hooting owl. Mewing? Pathetic. Brandy also did a lot of purring. It was possible that Brandy had a secret wish to be Catwoman, which, had it been explored by the author, might have made for a better read. But *mew* had earned a permanent place in their vocabulary.

She gave Jess the full story of the shift in behavior of—yes, her number one mew—Billy Gardiner: the vial, the wish, the *fascinating*, the unprecedented attention from Billy, the initial strong suspicion that something mean was being planned, the *let me come to homework club*, the *Hey, cool birdie*, the *I'm partners with Vân Ước*.

"Okay, let's get systematic. So—we know that magic wishes aren't a thing, right?" Jess gave her a look, as if checking to see that Vân Ước hadn't given up on the whole idea of sanity.

"Right."

"But we also know you are a smokin' babe, plus smart-as, and all things great…" Vân Ước shook her head in embarrassed denial, but before she had a chance to object, Jess continued, "Seeing as how I am the only lesbian-in-waiting present, I'm going to appoint myself as the expert on female beauty, so don't argue about *that*. The only question is, why now? And, given his track record of general meanness, I guess you were right to be suspicious about his motives. But that hasn't played out. So, what's the plan?"

"The plan? There is no plan. And his jokes are sometimes

long-term and quite elaborate, so that's still a definite possibility. So, there's just, how do I avoid him?"

"Nuh-uh. You're thinking public humiliation still likely, Billy-likes-Vân Ước long shot. Am I right?"

"Yeah."

"Whereas I'm thinking public humiliation long shot, Billy-likes-Vân Ước very likely."

"But I'm the only one present who has actually met Billy Gardiner, so I'm going to appoint myself as the expert on his behavior."

"Though you admit yourself that his behavior at the moment is uncharacteristic?"

"Bizarrely."

"So, your mission, if you choose to accept it, is to discover his true motivation."

Vân Ước picked up another rice cracker, scooped up some hummus, and crunched thoughtfully. "I guess."

"And how do you plan to do that?"

"Continued surveillance?"

"You need to step it up."

"What are you thinking?"

"Let him come to homework club, like he wants to."

"Really?"

"Show yourself to him, and see what he makes of the real you. Also, how else am I going to meet him?"

Jess was probably right. Homework club would at least let Billy see her in her own world.

Jess started laughing.

"What?"

"I'm just thinking, worst-case scenario, say he is a bastard, and he does try something mean—you'll get to use your favorite Jane quote."

Vân Ước laughed, too. And they said it together, in their best English accents. *"Do you think, because I am poor, obscure, plain, and little, I am soulless and heartless?—You think wrong!—I have as much soul as you,—and full as much heart!"*

It brought on a bad case of contagious giggles, and they were soon killing themselves laughing.

Fatal error. A banging on the wall started. The sounds of too much fun had filtered into the land of do-your-homework-study-hard.

Vân Ước got up, letting herself enjoy the lightness of heart that only came after a really good laugh with Jess, and left to face the music with her mother.

Walking along the corridor, she prepared herself for a talking-to about wasting valuable study time. She carefully stuffed her found cardigan into her backpack and unlocked the front door, wilting at the thought that she was going to get into trouble for messing around with Jess, as though she were a child, and yet she was also going to be the one checking up on her mother's medication—counting pills and taking responsibility for doctor's instructions being carried out, as though she were an adult.

She wouldn't mind having a run of just being a regular teenager.

11

Tuesday morning was TOK, Theory of Knowledge, another compulsory IB study unit. It was a kind of philosophy course.

Vân Uớc loved the content, but dreaded the nature of the class, which involved lots of public sharing of ideas and responses.

Today they were starting a unit looking at gender and society. Their teacher was Lucy Fraser. Dr. Fraser. She was one of the youngest members of staff, and a dynamo. She was wiry; she ran marathons; she hummed with energy. Her short hair was dyed electric orange, so she pretty much looked like a lit match. And right now she was telling the class, incandescent, evangelistic, about how the allocation of space in department stores was just one more manifestation of the pressures put on women to conform to external social constructs.

"Okay, let's take a walk through the most expensive retail real estate in this city. In *any* city. We're on the ground floor of David Jones, Saks, Harrods...What are the messages we're getting? And to whom are these messages being directed?"

"It's mostly women's cosmetics," offered Lou.

"Exactly," said Dr. Fraser.

Vân Ước hadn't really questioned the significance of this before, but it hit her like a cartoon anvil as Dr. Fraser continued. "And that prime real estate is overwhelmingly dedicated to letting women know that they don't measure up. Your skin, your lips, your nails—they're not the right color; you don't smell right; you're too wrinkly; too oily; too dry. Why have we signed on for this?"

People were yawning, making some notes, checking Facebook, happy for Dr. Fraser to do all the work.

"Now let's imagine walking through that same space and seeing the entire ground floor gender-flipped—all the products are dedicated to making men feel less-than. Men, *you* need this panoply, you get to choose from a hundred different varieties of black paste to wipe on your eyelashes, makeup to change your skin color, blush to give you an outdoor glow, age-minimizing, pore-minimizing, lip-maximizing, petroleum-based...crap. Why doesn't the picture look like that?"

"Until recently women had no power," said Sibylla. "They didn't have the vote. They couldn't inherit or own land. They'd usually be dependent on their partner or their father. And they'd attract a husband partly because of how they looked. So maybe the emphasis on women's appearance is still a relic from that era."

"Yes. Women have had less power historically. Let's look at the reasons behind that—what are some of the most obvious ones?" She was greeted with silence. "Come on, has everyone done the reading for this class?"

"There's only been reliable contraception for about the last fifty years," said Lou.

Dr. Fraser nodded. "In the scheme of things, control of fertility is a very recent gain. And remember, too, that dependence on men, on fathers, brothers, husbands, was enshrined in law. When did women get the vote? When were they enfranchised? Not until 1902. If you were an indigenous woman, or man, not till 1962." That elicited some shocked gasps. "What year could married women own land in Australia? It was 1879. When did they have rights over children in the event of a marriage being dissolved? 1839. When did rape within marriage stop being a legal right of a husband? In 1991, in England, and has not stopped yet in 144 countries. Right now."

Dr. Fraser paused to let it all sink in. Vân Ước looked around. Most people were now paying attention.

"All the stats about income and stuff like domestic violence show that women are definitely still oppressed. But I still want to paint my toenails sometimes," said Sibylla.

Dr. Fraser smiled. "Me too. We're part of a complex pattern. What are some of the primary shapers of the pattern?"

Vân Ước looked at Billy. Right away he looked up, made eye

contact. She felt the heat rising to the surface of her skin. She looked down. But she couldn't help herself; she glanced up again and Billy was still looking at her, smiling in a wondering way. Huh, wonder away. It was nothing compared to her level of wondering. *What* was going on in his head?

The conversation roamed through economics, social norms, intersectionality, and the history of the women's movement. They left with a reminder from Dr. Fraser to look at the Mary Wollstonecraft readings on the subject portal and come to the next class ready to contribute.

● ● ●

She managed to dodge Billy for the rest of the day, and he wasn't in the locker area after school. But Holly was.

"Well, well, little Van Truck, the girl with wheels—and wings."

Vân Ước gave what she hoped was a neutral glance at the group—Holly, Gabi, Tiff. All the hair-flicking and leaning and artfully combining poses made it look as though there must be a photographer around to shoot them at any moment. Because there was a photographer around to shoot them. One of them always had a phone stuck out at arm's length, while each performed their face of the moment. They all checked out the image; each had veto power if it was a horrible picture of any one of them. But they were all such adept posers it was never horrible. They all put themselves down, expecting with full confidence that their friends would deny the false deprecation.

I look like shit. Omigod, that is such crap, you are so gorgeous I hate you. A Botticelli-esque photo would capture them perfectly. In their uniforms, but posed as the Three Graces in *Primavera*. Billy could be the youth plucking an orange from the tree. It had the potential to say something about their self-importance, their inflated view of themselves, when, after all, they were just kids at school, not so different from lots of kids at lots of schools. It made her smile.

"Ooh, she's smiling at us. She thinks, 'Billy called *my cardigan* cute, so now these gals are my pals,'" Holly said.

Vân Ước packed her bag as quickly as she could without looking like she wanted to run away.

Holly walked over to her. "Are you deaf?"

"No."

"Where did you buy the cardigan that Billy pretended he liked yesterday?"

She zipped her backpack, swung it onto her shoulders, and tried to leave, but Holly blocked her path.

"I didn't hear an answer."

She decided to tell the truth. "I found it."

"You *found* it? You mean you stole it?"

"No."

Holly stepped back as though Vân Ước were suddenly contagious, or smelled bad.

"Why do they let people like that in?" said Tiff.

"It's not even fair to *them*," added Gabi.

Vân Ước walked out, silently cursing Billy for shining this unwanted light on her. She didn't need the stress.

•••

She'd walked off some of her anger by the time she reached the river, when she heard the troublemaker's voice right behind her.

"Wait up, Vân Ước." Billy jumped off his bike and was beside her before she could cross the road, detonate her backpack, or put on her invisibility cloak. So she looked at the footpath. Looking down. Don't knock it. It could be useful. It was the source of all the ideas she was developing for her portfolio. Billy leaned down and down until his face was in her eye line.

"Yes?"

"Which way are you heading?"

She nodded in the direction of the river.

"Can I walk with you?"

"You've got your bike; it'd be quicker..." *If you jumped on it, and disappeared.*

"But I want to speak to you."

"Don't you have to be somewhere else?" *Get. Lost.*

He was gazing at her in an extremely disconcerting way.

"It's just, you said Friday is your only nontraining day. And it's Tuesday."

He checked his watch. "Shit—sorry, you're right. I do have to go."

But he wasn't budging. He was just looking at her.

"What?"

"Do you want to come, too?"

A third theory occurred to her. Billy wasn't in a wish-induced spell. There was never any joke with her as the punch line. He'd simply, and totally, lost the plot.

"Come with you to rowing training?"

"Yeah, and then maybe we could hang out."

"I have stuff to do." That was true. There was always stuff.

"Sure. So, the other thing was, did you ask at your tutoring program if I can come join?"

"Well…" She remembered Jess's advice. It was certainly one way to flush out exactly what was going on. And he'd still need to have the Working with Children check done, so that would take a couple of weeks, and by then it might all have resolved itself one way or the other.

"Well?" Billy gave her his most dazzling smile as he straightened his front wheel, forearms leaning on handlebars.

"Okay. You can come for a tryout and meet the coordinator—*after* you get a Working with Children check."

"Cool. I'll come on Friday, then—I've already got my check from running the nippers program at the surf lifesaving club over summer."

Damn it. Her buffer zone vaporized and floated skyward. "All right."

"So, see you then. See you tomorrow, actually. In math."

"Sure."

"And English practice? Not tomorrow, but *next* Wednesday at mine should work."

"I can't. I've got oboe class."

"And I've got training. So after—okay?"

"Okay."

She continued across the river, her shoes tapping out *damn it damn it damn it damn it.*

The billboards on the Albert Street corner sang their usual song: *Thin is good. Half naked is good. Blonde is good. White is good.* But today, instead of it being semi-invisible wallpaper or a mild annoyance, a space from which she expected to be excluded, Vân Ước found herself thinking, *Fuck you, advertisers, get your freaking photoshopped sexist Anglo-normative ideas about beauty out of my face.*

That put a spring in her step. For starters, she only said *fuck* in her silent ranting. And it felt good. Second, she wasn't in the habit of speaking out against blatant everyday racism, such as the always-all-white dominance of every beauty advertisement and fashion magazine around, except if there was an ethnic Other-ing erotic/exotic angle, then, sure, cast Asian. Although why should having the right words to express her annoyance *to herself* make the annoyance feel any less annoying? The silent rebel. Woo.

Maybe it was just Dr. Fraser's contagious passion about not accepting all the messages that are shoved in the collective female face. Be skeptical. Ask why. She gave you the feeling that you could do something to change the world. That what you thought mattered. And that felt powerful. It was like what had happened physically at Mount Fairweather. Her body had changed—she'd become fitter, stronger, tougher.

Maybe, eventually, she'd also have some more muscle in the way she dealt with the world. She'd be able to live up to the *What would Jane do?* standard, not just the *I know what Jane would do, but I can't actually do it* standard.

12

Once she was home and waiting for the elevator to groan its way down to pick her up in the ground-floor lobby, she was hit by a half-formed worry lurching into uncomfortable focus. Billy was just like those billboard girls, wasn't he? Couldn't she see him up there in some Calvin Klein boxers? He wouldn't even need photoshopping. He looked unbelievably good in just his bike shorts. Wasn't he the most conforming version of blond Anglo male beauty she'd ever seen in real life? Had she internalized a paradigm she should be questioning or, better still, outright rejecting? Too late for a political lightbulb moment now. Her imagination had signed on from the moment she first saw him without clearing it with her brain, and since then she'd become

just as interested in whatever was brooding away under the surface as she was in the beautiful surface itself.

• • •

Unlocking the front door, she stepped right into double-uh-oh
land.

Uh-oh number one: no smell of cooking; no sign of food
preparation. Uh-oh number two: neat stacks of cut-out garments still sitting in taped plastic bags on the kitchen bench.

She had hoped they'd prevent it this year, but maybe not—
maybe they'd hit a speed bump that was too high and rolled
backward.

When Dr. Chin had confirmed the post-traumatic stress
disorder diagnosis, he'd gone through the treatment in detail:
antidepressants and therapy. But because her mother had
stopped feeling well, got careless with the tablet-taking, and
had not increased the dose as she'd been instructed to...here
they were again.

She could see why the worst time for her mother each year
coincided with the anniversary of the boat journey from Vietnam, and how the PTSD had become a monster, ready to burst
forth each year, still ravenous. But she also imagined that
whatever her mother had witnessed, whatever she'd experienced, was with her every day. Every morning when she woke
up. Every evening when she tried to sleep. What did she see?
Vân Ước longed to know, and at the same time half hoped

never to know. She wondered if the nightmares of her imagination came close to her parents' experience.

Under the doctor's direction, and with her father's agreement, Vân Ước had partly bossed and partly cajoled her mother into agreeing to attend group therapy with other women who'd made the journey. The conversation had gone something like this:

"Ma, Dr. Chin says there's a group of women who meet and talk to each other about leaving Vietnam."

"Why would anyone want to do that?"

"It's run by that social worker—you know Như Mai? Who visits people here? And she brings families to homework club sometimes? You've met her. She's nice."

"Why is it her business to get everyone to talk about this? And why are you telling me?"

"Because it might help you to go along. Dr. Chin said you should go."

"I'm not going anywhere. I don't know these people."

"It could be that some of your friends will be there."

"My friends and I don't need to talk. We got out. And we got on with things."

"You didn't have any counseling when you arrived, though, did you?"

"Counseling?"

Vân Ước hadn't used quite the right word in Vietnamese. "You know what I mean—talking through your problems." She was trying not to sound impatient or disrespectful.

"Sounds like a waste of time. If you survive, your problems are gone."

So many of her mother's family members had died, it was hard to argue: if you survived, your problems *were* gone. The most pressing one, anyway: how to stay alive.

But her mother had been going to group therapy for a couple of months now and was, for her, pretty positive about it.

Vân Ước went quietly into her parents' room, in case her mother was asleep.

She wasn't sleeping. She was staring at the ceiling.

Sitting down lightly on the bed, Vân Ước took her mother's hand. "Mama? Are you okay?"

"Vân Ước, *con*."

Con meant "child" but with overtones of something like "little one"; it was an affectionate greeting, in any case, so she took courage. "Mama, you're not feeling well? I'm bringing in your tablets."

"Leave them. They don't work."

"Dr. Chin told you—you have to keep taking them, and increase the dose to make sure they keep working. Today we'll start again. I'm making another appointment for you to see him. We're going to do what he says, and stick with these tablets."

Her mother rolled her head away. "You treat me like a child."

"I'm trying to look after you well, like a mother, like you look after me."

"I don't need it. I am the mother."

"But you still need help sometimes."

During exchanges like this, Vân Ước had to try to forget the frequent, imperious command *Do for me!* (read something, explain to someone, pay a bill, make a complaint, speak on the phone, give technical advice…), which didn't fit so well with *I am the mother*. Her mother never acknowledged these inconsistencies.

The expression on her face was mutinous. She was strong-willed. And that didn't change when she was unwell.

"What about when *I* am a doctor?" Vân Ước asked, mentally crossing her fingers for peddling the family dream when she had no intention of making good on it.

Aha. The wedge. Her mother was smiling.

"If you work hard enough. Study hard. We will be so proud of our daughter. You will live in a big house, in Kew."

"And I will make people well?"

"You will have a waiting room full of people who come to be cured."

"And I will expect all my patients to take their tablets that I carefully prescribe for them."

Her mother's lips were firmly closed again.

"Won't I? Mama, think about it—you know it's true."

"Maybe."

"So…"

"So you will be better than Dr. Chin. You will only prescribe the tablets that work."

"These tablets will work, if you just keep taking them. No skipping a day. You won't feel better straightaway after the dose changes. Remember him explaining that to us?"

"They want our money for tablets that don't even work."

"They just work in a different, slower way. And then they

make you feel better for a long time. *But only if you keep taking them.*" Vân Ước got up to leave.

"You and Daddy will do the sewing today."

Great, that would poke a big hole into homework time. So apparently some time wasting was permissible. Just nothing fun. Hanging out with Jess: no. Slave labor: yes. But her mother looked sad and ashamed; Vân Ước didn't have the heart to let her annoyance show.

"We can do it. And I'll call and cancel for the rest of the week. You just rest."

She went out into the hallway, took a deep breath in order not to scream, went into the bathroom, and saw her own face in the mirrored cabinet. Worried. And pissed off. She'd have to get dinner organized, too. She fished around the narrow shelves and found the right box. Fortunately her mother was too tight with money to chuck stuff out once she'd paid for it. Vân Ước checked the dose, popped two white pills out, filled a glass of water, and closed the cabinet door. She checked her reflection again, removed worried, removed pissed off, put on confident, added a touch of positive, and headed back into the bedroom.

13

The common room was a new privilege, just for years eleven
and twelve. Each year level had its own room, in different
buildings, and people used them to have lunch in if the weather
was bad, or as a place to hang out during a spare period; some
people—the ones with a high noise tolerance—even worked
in there. They were allowed to play music, and there was a
massive bulletin board where people could post "appropriate"
material.

School had tried to make the common room feel like a relaxing retreat. They'd even used the word *chill* in the literature,
which was unfortunate. Sofas and comfy chairs and coffee
tables had been donated by students' parents, creating a mis-
matched informality. A teakettle, a microwave oven, a fridge,

and a sandwich press made for more comforting food options than the usual lunchbox fare.

The room overlooked a small garden area, a dead-end wedge created when the new library building (the Redmond Information and Technology Center) was connected to one of the old buildings. It had a low-grade background smell of instant noodles and bananas, which wasn't unpleasant, but which, over time, they would no doubt come to associate with the stressful work requirements of the year.

The one thing that no one liked about the common room was that it had a CCTV security camera in one corner of the ceiling. Cameras were dotted all over the school, but it seemed like an invasion to have one right inside this particular room.

Pippa, whose older sisters had all gone through the school, always had the scoop on the whys, wherefores, and deep history. She said, *They had no choice—it was just a smokers' den before the camera went in. I guess they were worried they'd be sued for passive smoking injury.*

Vân Ước had to steel herself to go into the common room. She wouldn't have bothered if it hadn't been for the CCTV camera. Her scholarship was for general excellence, and that had a community component. Imagine if someone checked through the footage and noticed that she never went into the most community-specific space that the school had created for her year level. On one hand it was ridiculous to think that anyone had the time to waste on a check like that. On the other hand, why not play it safe? She was used to jumping through hoops that were put in front of her.

The room didn't feel like hers in any way. It was a distillation of the exclusion she expected to feel, a concentration of the in-ness of various friendship groups. Worse than walking out into the playground glare of unpopularity, here you had to walk through a doorway. All eyes flicked up upon each entry. People were greeted with enthusiasm. Room was made for them to sit down. Or, in cases like hers, eyes flicked down again, and the silence screamed in her ears. It wasn't that she minded it particularly, but she did mind other people witnessing it. And she dreaded teachers getting wind of it, and maybe finding awful, inventive ways for her to join in more effectively. She had decided her strategy would be to make a cup of tea—BYO tea bags—and sit down and pretend to study, or really study if that were at all possible.

So before class, on this hot and thundery Wednesday, a week into term, she made her second visit to the common room. Disturbing sounds of occupation and hilarity were bubbling into the corridor. Fun? It wasn't much past 8 a.m. A couple of lengths of the corridor, arm swinging and deep breathing, and she dived in. Not a splashy dive from a height, more like entering already underwater and hoping not to be noticed. But rather than being able to make her way inconspicuously to the coffee- and tea-making area, she was immediately pounced on by Billy. Not physically—he was standing at the most centrally located coffee table in the middle of a Jenga battle with Vincent.

He called from the door, "Vân Ước, come over here."

She froze.

"Vân Ước!"

The whole room was quiet. Billy's friends looked at him like, *What? Why the sudden interest in her?* They were as mystified as she was. Her couple of scholarship cronies shrank as deeply into their seats as possible, hoping not to be called on for any impossible rescues.

Billy looked around. "Hey, I like the silence—finally some attention. Because I've got an announcement..." He turned a slow circle, making sure everyone was looking at him.

Might she actually throw up, right here, right now? Please, no. Her eyes flicked around nervously. Where was someone like Lou when you needed her?

Billy continued, "Vincent Linus Cronin is about to eat a dick." He looked at the Jenga tower with complete concentration, slowly pulled out a rod without causing the structure to crash, and roared with satisfaction. Vincent was sweating—they really took it this seriously? He removed the next rod. The tower remained standing.

"And that was his undoing..." Billy looked around for her again. "Vân Ước, come over and help me—I need physics expertise for my final move."

Billy's friends—and particularly Holly—were again doing a double take. She walked over to the game and stood nearby. What was she going to do? Withhold a Jenga opinion?

"Thank you!" said Billy. "I'm thinking this one." He pointed to a rod down toward the base layer. Vân Ước did a quick assessment of the structure and nodded. It was the one she'd choose.

It was as though one of her weird Billy dreams had come to

life: Billy noticing her. Billy talking to her. Billy wanting her opinion. Everyone seeing that Billy liked her.

Billy extracted the rod. And again, the structure held.

"You're fucked now, buddy," he said to Vincent, who clearly agreed, admitting defeat in a sour smirk.

Vincent pulled a rod out, and the edifice went smashing down over the coffee table, spilling onto the floor. Billy stretched both arms up, triumphant. He punched his own chest. "Jenga king," he yelled. People laughed, rolled their eyes. Everyone was used to his hyperexuberance. He turned to Vân Ước, punching the air and chanting, "I am the Jenga king. I am the JENGA KING."

She flinched; it was as though he were about to charge through her, but instead he picked her up, spun her around in a circle, put her down again, and continued his lap of triumph around the common room. He stacked two chairs on the table closest to the CCTV camera, climbed up them, and said into the camera: "I AM JENGA in this school!"

"Dude, there's no audio," said Ben.

"Then they can READ MY LIPS," Billy shouted into the camera before jumping down, chairs crashing behind him.

By now everyone was laughing—except Vân Ước. She couldn't decide whether fury or mortification would win the day. Whatever Billy Gardiner's game was, and however she fitted into it, she wasn't available to be picked up and put down like a doll. She forgot about her cup of tea and walked out.

When Billy called to her, she was striding through the parking lot near the science building and still angry.

The morning's rain had eased, but it was warm and thundery still; lightning arced and flicked across the mauve-clouded sky.

He caught up to her. "Why'd you run off? You brought me good luck."

"Why are you following me around? Why are you speaking to me out of the blue like this?" she asked him.

"Why wouldn't I?"

"Because you never have before. You didn't even seem to know who I was until last week."

"So, call me stupid. I know who you are now."

"Good, then you can leave me alone now."

A fork of lightning flashed bright white nearby, and between them, right onto the hood of Dr. Fraser's silver hybrid, a bird fell with a thud, dead, its tiny bundle of entrails exploded out, a thread of smoke rising in a spiral from its broken chest.

"SHIIIIIT!" said Billy. "Wow. How cool is that?"

She couldn't believe her ears. He thought it was *cool* that a small bird got electrocuted right in front of them? Just great. She had a psychopath following her around.

14

Art class that afternoon was devoted to journaling.

As part of their assessment, each student would be required to present a document demonstrating the thought processes and practical studies and explorations behind the portfolio pieces. Ms. Halabi said that, ideally, the journal should strike a balance between playground and laboratory. She also warned the class that examiners could always tell if a journal had been put together at the last minute. Even though it seemed like a soft-option part of the course, it had to be undertaken seriously.

The teacher went quietly from student to student to chat, still getting to know them all, while Vân Ước worked on a journal page devoted to the artist Elizabeth Gower, and specifically to the jewel-bright mosaics Gower made from product labels and packaging.

"Aha," said Ms. Halabi. "So tell me how this relates to your work."

"It's the beauty of the overlooked object...an article I read talked about constructing an aesthetic from the mundane."

"And what does the artist have to say about it?"

"She—for her it's political, too. Questioning consumerism."

"Okay. And you're giving your work some more thought?"

Vân Ước nodded, but she'd had no new insights since Friday.

"Remember to keep investigating—*What does it mean?* and *What does it mean to me?*"

It felt amazing to have her work taken seriously, to be treated like an artist. She was buzzing with adrenaline and—she had to admit it—she enjoyed the added thrill that this was hers alone, a secret life. Secret from her parents, anyway. That felt heady, addictive. Maybe there was an element she wasn't so proud of: *Keep your secrets about our family; I've got my own secrets.*

As she left the art room, Holly walked up alongside her, lightly bumping her, smiling. "Go look at the bulletin board, bitch."

Vân Ước knew that smile, and her euphoria evaporated. She'd gone from the category of ignored/despised to being squarely in Holly's sights. Thanks, Billy. The old dudes were at her shoulder, naturally. *She's full of herself today/Who does she think she is?/Of course she's heading for a fall/What did she expect?*

• • •

The dilemma was whether to go to the common room now and see what Holly was talking about, or wait and try to go in at a less crowded time. At least Holly wouldn't be there now; she'd been heading in the opposite direction. Perhaps she'd check out the lay of the land, and have a covert look at the board.

She expected the worst and wasn't disappointed. A photo of her in the rainbow-wing cardigan, blown up and printed on six A4 sheets of paper, with the caption, SECURITY WARNING: CERTAIN PEOPLE WEAR STOLEN GOODS. LOCK UP YOUR POSSESSIONS.

People who'd been at the board, obviously looking at the pictures of her, drifted away, leaving her uncertain of what her rights were here, and what she should do. If she took them down, would it make her look more guilty, or less? Would there be any point? Holly could just print more.

What would Jane do? Jane had been humiliated unfairly at school. She'd been punished and called a liar in front of her whole class. Then she'd cried. Even Jane was only human.

Vân Ước had the horrible, rare, and certain feeling that *she* was about to cry. She headed out quickly, brushing past Lou, Sibylla, and Billy, running across the colonnade to the library and down the stairs to the basement level. There she shoved open two sets of swinging doors, and locked herself in a bathroom stall.

She sat down and let the crying hit her. It was powerful and engulfing, and she knew from experience that it would take a while for her to resurface. She wasn't a crier. Once, maybe twice a year she'd have a good howl. So when she did cry, she was overloaded, like a storm cloud, and miseries came pouring out in a torrent.

Her anxiety about her mother (Why couldn't she have a capable, happy mother who looked after *her*, instead of vice versa?); her frustration that her father didn't get more involved, wasn't better at helping her mother; her confusion about Billy Gardiner; and all the rest of her current-release poor-me catalog items—no money, no designer clothes, no nice clothes even, people would believe she stole something because she was poor, parents didn't even speak the language, no nice place to live, parents wouldn't even apply to live in one of the *real houses with a garden* that the housing commission owned, parents had no car, she'd never been out of the country, never had a pet (unless you counted a succession of former goldfish, which she didn't), always had to be on her best behavior because of the scholarship, must look like a craven approval seeker, no friends at school, wouldn't get into art school even with a good portfolio because she'd be tongue-tied and too shy to talk about the work in interviews, never had a boyfriend, would never have a boyfriend, only ever had one (fake) Barbie (with cheap hair that matted) when she was little.

Finally there flowed the generalized sorry-for-selfness that was virtually forbidden in her life, but which flavored it completely, or maybe just reduced her life's flavor overall, about not being allowed to be unhappy about any bloody thing because if you *survived*, then you were all right; no—*lucky*. What problems? You're alive! She wanted more than survival. She wanted beauty; she wanted love; she wanted *abundance*.

Why was it okay for everyone around her to have more than enough, but she had to be content with less?

Her whole body was crying now, shoulders and chest heaving, tears streaming, running down her neck, making the collar of her dress wet, nose running. She was a big, snotty pile of self-pity. And she despised herself almost as much as she pitied herself. What a pathetic weakling. Now she would be red-eyed, flushed, and blotchy for the rest of the day and *everyone would know she'd been crying*, and then they'd all think she was guilty.

She was shocked into stopping, with a gulp, when the door into the bathroom opened. She flushed the toilet to cover the noise she was making, drew a deep breath through sobs still galloping to get out, yanked down some toilet paper, and blew her nose. But didn't open the door. She hiccuped.

"Vân Ước?"

Crap. Was there no getting away from him? She hiccuped again.

"Look, I know it's you."

"This is the girls' bathroom."

"Yeah, it's just you and me, though, so I figured it was okay."

"It's not."

"I heard you crying."

"Can you please go?"

"I just want to make sure you're okay."

"I'm okay." Hiccup.

"You don't sound it. What's with the stuff on the bulletin board?"

"I don't know."

Vân Ước heard the noise of a toilet seat banging shut.

"You're not actually *using* the toilet now, are you?" Billy asked.

"No."

"Cool."

She looked up. He was standing on the toilet in the next stall, looking down at her. She had a momentary sense of disbelief that she had ever, *ever* wished for Billy Gardiner to notice her.

The door to the bathroom opened again, and she heard murmurs as two more people came in.

"What the fuck are you doing up there?"

Thank god. It was Lou. Not that Vân Ước wanted to see anyone. But she had no confidence that she could get rid of Billy alone.

"Get lost, Billy," Sibylla said.

He jumped back down. "Do you want me to stay, Vân Ước?"

"NO."

"Okay, I'll see you in class."

The door opened and closed again. She assumed Billy was gone.

"Are you okay?" asked Lou.

Vân Ước was still trying to get her breathing and sobbing under control. "Sure," she said, sounding only a bit quaky.

"I'm getting eye drops," Sibylla said. "I'll be back."

"What's going on?" Lou asked when Sibylla had gone. "What's the thing on the bulletin board about?"

Vân Ước opened the door and saw how bad she must look reflected in Lou's sympathetic face a beat before she saw herself in the mirror. "Oh no."

"Don't worry, Sib'll be back soon. Splash your face with cold water, and we'll talk."

15

It was such a relief to tell Sibylla and Lou the true story of the winged cardigan, even through the hiccups and sobs that continued while her body recovered from the crying storm.

In her measured way, Lou looked at Vân Ước. "I know you don't like talking, but you have to let people know how you found the cardigan."

"It's a cool story. It must be someone's art/life/fashion project," said Sibylla.

Seeing the sense in telling everyone her side of the story was one thing; being able to do it would require her to speak to people. Major impediment.

Sibylla frowned. "The first thing we do is rip down what's on the board. And if Holly prints more and puts them back up, we tell Ms. King."

"Or at least tell Holly that we'll tell her," said Lou.

"Which brings us to why she's being such a complete bitch to you," said Sibylla. "It's obviously Billy. You're stepping on her territory. More so since they hooked up recently. Not that that means anything. To him, anyway. But there's no way she's going to welcome you into the fold."

"I mean, are you in the fold?" Lou wanted to know. "Is there something happening with you and Billy?"

Vân Ước shook her head. "I have no idea why he's—"

"Climbing onto toilets to talk to you?"

"He's just... I don't think he even knew who I was last term, and now he's following me around." Saying it out loud didn't make it seem any more plausible.

"Not that you're not crush-worthy, Vân Ước. But it is a bit weird," said Lou.

"It's just that Billy's..." Sibylla paused, looking worried.

"A dick," Lou finished.

"He's so used to everyone thinking he's this great guy, he's funny, he's popular, that he'll happily trample over anyone to get a laugh and not even notice that he's done any damage."

"He's like a really annoying puppy—he chewed your shoes but, oh, look, he's still wagging his tail. Remember how he went on and on about your big undies, Sib?"

Sibylla smacked her forehead in mock despair. He'd continued a *once seen, never forgotten* series of gags about her knickers for the whole time they were at Mount Fairweather, Vân Ước remembered. "He's a guy who doesn't give a shit about collateral damage if he gets a laugh."

"Did you hear he set up a fake Crowthorne Grammar School e-mail account last year and sent a pile of e-mails that looked like they came from the year-ten coordinator to all his friends' parents, complaining of—what was it?—*lackluster* academic performance, and encouraging them to set more rigorous study timetables at home," said Lou.

Vân Ước couldn't help smiling. It was pretty funny. But that sort of prank didn't happen on the spur of the moment. It took some planning.

"Also, he's never really had what I would call a relationship," said Sibylla. "He periodically succumbs to being someone's boyfriend, so long as they do all the work and don't make any demands."

"And I think we've all heard the revolting line he uses about rowing: 'oars before whores'?" said Lou.

"Gross," said Vân Ước. It really was. In which case, why, since she first laid eyes on him, and despite everything she'd since discovered about him, had he been the one to persistently invade her daydreams?

"I mean, I guess the message is, keep your guard up. Whatever he's up to, following you around like you're his new hobby, he's never shown himself to be good boyfriend material," said Sibylla.

"Bottom line, he's your standard-issue two-dimensional hot jock, and you can do better," said Lou.

What *was* Billy up to? He certainly had no history of interest in a girl on the outermost ring of the social circle. In fact, even the inner-sanctum girls had a hard time getting quality attention from him. And if it was the wish—*it couldn't be the wish*—shouldn't she hear a shimmer of fairy bells or something every time he came near?

They kept chatting as they headed upstairs, by which time a quick check in the mirror showed Vân Ước that her eyes were brightly vasoconstricted white, thanks to Sibylla's drops, and her face only a little bit blotchy.

16

After the horror she had not sought to hide following the fried bird incident, after the firm *go away* message in the library bathroom, after successfully dodging Billy all day Thursday—the one day they didn't have a class together—Vân Ước was astounded to see him front up to homework club on Friday. He hadn't even double-checked the time or location with her. She assumed he'd forgotten. But he just strolled in, right on time, relaxed, confidently scoping the room.

It was awful, truly awful, that even though her official response was horrified, her heart betrayed her with a distinct skippety-thud when he arrived. She made eye contact with Jess and nodded in his direction. Jess took one look at him and mouthed *wow*, eyebrows up. He was a showstopper in the looks department, no doubt about it.

He saw Vân Ước and sauntered over, deftly weaving his way around the tables, chairs, and wandering kids.

Jess had been making a beeline for Vân Ước as soon as she realized that Billy was Billy. They arrived at the same time.

"Billy, Jess; Jess, Billy," Vân Ước said.

"Hi," said Jess.

"Hi," he replied, not really looking at Jess.

Vân Ước looked from Jess to Billy and back again, hoping one of them would say something. Billy stared at Vân Ước, ignoring Jess. Jess looked at Billy and clocked that she was being ignored. She crossed her eyes and pulled a Jess face, and still Billy didn't glance at her.

And, hello, this was familiar. As soon as Billy had said his perfunctory *hi* to Jess, his eyes had skated right over her, through her, as though she were a chair or a rock. He'd made a summary assessment: She was a nobody. An irrelevance. Vân Ước's heart sank. This was exactly how Billy had looked at her until a week and a half ago. It wasn't malevolent; it was simply a case of utter disregard. It guaranteed that Jess would not be remembered next time they met. Jess was a sharp-looking girl—and, more important, smart, funny, and nice. Plus, she was a *human being* who deserved his attention, and his courtesy.

That careless, disrespectful arrogance rekindled the anger in Vân Ước's heart. She made sure she kept her distance from Billy as she led him over to meet Eleanor.

Oh, it was nauseating. The eye contact. The firm handshake. The warm smile. Eleanor's *Oh, you must be Jonathan's son.* The brief summary of the summer's volunteer work at the lifesaving club. The reference from the club's president. Eleanor gave Billy a form to fill out and welcomed him on board.

"Vân Ước, given Billy's background with younger children and sports, I think I'll put him with you and preps, ones, and twos—on playground duty. Can you make sure he settles in?"

"Sure," Vân Ước said.

"Do whatever Vân Ước tells you, Billy—she's the boss. We couldn't manage around here without her."

Vân Ước smiled at Eleanor, in spite of being freshly lumbered with Billy, whom she had assumed would be assigned an older student and be sent upstairs, where she need not cross paths with him.

Billy turned away from Eleanor, expecting Vân Ước to lead them back to the small kids' area, but at the same time a boy behind Vân Ước pulled out his chair and trapped her into staying where she was. So, as Billy stepped toward her, she was sandwiched between his body and the chair. The surge of sensation that shot through her was so extreme she felt like a pinball machine on tilt. Billy's *whoa*, and *sorry*, and step backward to give her some room was all that stopped her from throwing her arms around him.

She frowned at the insistent kaleidoscope of romance cover–worthy images flipping through her mind and gave herself a mental smack on the head. This was a boy she did not particularly trust. He was going to be working for her here. That was all. At school she would continue to do her best to avoid him, and with any luck he'd eventually leave her alone.

She pushed the obstructing chair back in and led Billy to the front of the church hall. She turned back to check that he was following, and he gave her the most confident, amused smile she'd ever seen. A smile that surely said he had felt what she had felt—or maybe it said he had read her mind and knew what she was thinking about. The smile distracted her again and redirected heat flow. She took a deep breath. Maybe mewing wasn't so unbelievable after all. Maybe Billy Gardiner produced the sort of sparks that meant a mew was some kind of scientific inevitability. She almost laughed out loud; that was ridiculous. They reached the side door nearest to the playground. "Okay, brace yourself."

Vân Ước introduced him to a few of the little kids. Mahad and Barney immediately involved him in a hot dispute as to which of them had farted.

"You farted!"

"I did not. *You* farted."

"Did not; you did."

"You stink."

"No, *you* stink."

Just when things were about to boil over, Billy intervened. "Who mentioned the fart first?"

Mahad pointed at Barney.

"Okay," said Billy, his manner serious. "You work out the fart fight using ancient wisdom: 'A fox smells its own scent first.' And in addition to that: 'He who smelt it, dealt it.' Barney, you farted."

"Okay, I did!" said Barney.

The boys burst out laughing and ran over to the cobweb-shaped climbing frame, shouting to each other. "He who smelt it, dealt it!"

Billy smiled at Vân Ước, a self-satisfied look on his face.

"Yep, you fit right in here," she said, heading back into the church hall.

17

Vân Ước tidied up the little kids' area after homework club. She liked the routine: putting the pencils back in their jars, stacking the unused paper, clipping the lids on the modeling-clay containers, tidying the books away into the book bins, and making sure the gym mats where the kids lounged around and read were free of any sticky spills.

She took her time more than usual just to make sure that Billy would be long gone by the time she headed home. She sprayed and wiped down the tables (not even her job) before she got her bag, said good-bye to the church custodian, Serena, who locked up each week, and opened the door into the still-hot afternoon.

Oh, great. Billy was sitting on a swing, texting. He looked up at the sound of the door, came over, and started unlocking his bike. Vân Ước kept walking.

"Wait up, I'll walk you home."

"I can get there by myself."

He wasn't that easily put off. He walked along beside her, wheeling his bike, ignoring the periodic buzzing of his phone. "Which way are we heading?"

"I only live about five minutes away; I really don't need..."

"You were great in there," he said. "You know every kid. How long have you been doing this?"

"Just since last year." Despite having done what Jess suggested, and letting him come along to see her in her natural habitat, he had no real idea of who she was. It was time to take the plunge. This would be sure to get rid of him. "Before then, I was a student here. I've been coming here every week since year five. My parents hardly speak any English. We live in the high-rise public housing, like most of the kids who come here. Tutors, like you are now, go home to Toorak. Students, like I was, go home to the apartments."

Billy stared at her. "Cool. So at least I know I'm heading in the right direction."

Huh? He hadn't skipped a beat. Did he already know? She glanced at him. He was wandering along, appearing not to have a care in the world. His phone buzzed again. He took it out of his pocket, read the screen, and sighed.

"Are you going to Tiff's tonight?"

"Ah—no. We're not friends."

"Yeah, I don't want to go, either. Only it's her birthday

drinks. So I should. I guess. But why? Why do I have to do all this stuff?"

"Because she's your friend?"

"Yeah, but not really. And I have to be up at five."

"So, maybe—go home now?" He really stuck around like glue, and didn't take a hint.

Billy smiled at her. "But this is the best part of my day so far."

"You must have had a pretty ordinary day."

"Can we go back to your place and hang for a while?"

Vân Ước looked at him. He did not seem to be joking. "No. We can't. My mother's not well."

"Hey, I'm sorry. What's wrong?"

"She . . . I'm not sure that she'd want me talking about it."

"No, cool. I'm sorry. Hope she feels better soon."

They were at the gates of the apartment complex. "Okay, bye," said Vân Ước.

"See you on Monday," Billy said, wheeling his bike away with a plausible impression of regret as Matthew walked up, wearing his ever-present, genuine—as he was keen to point out, though who cared?—French beret, whistling tunelessly between his teeth, and greeting Vân Ước with a familiar *yo*.

• • •

Jess broke up a block of Turkish delight chocolate, her confectionery mew, looking very stern.

"Billy. Huh. What an arrogant, self-centered dick," she said. "He was strutting around like he owned the place. First visit!"

"That's typical behavior."

"Well, I can't see why he's your mew guy." Jess ate a piece of chocolate. "Except for he's magazino handsome."

"Yeah."

"And cut. He must do nothing but work out."

"He's the stroke of the first eight."

"Which means?"

"It means when he's not studying, he's training. It's the top position in the school's best rowing crew."

"Right."

"Which he holds in year eleven—so, he's the king of rowing a year earlier than you might expect."

"So, he can *row very quickly*? Big deal. He's not good enough for you."

"What did you think? I mean, did you get a sense of what he thinks about me?"

"He's besotted, you idiot. You have won the heart of one very hot dickhead."

Frowning to hide her annoyingly automatic thrilled response, Vân Ước pressed play on their Friday movie, *Clueless*, which they hadn't seen since last year. "That was way harsh, Tai," she said.

"Not even a quarter of the harsh he deserves. Seriously, we couldn't be friends if you went out with him."

"Our friendship is safe."

Vân Ước reached for a piece of the Turkish delight chocolate, which made her think of Narnia, of bewitchment, and of little glass vials.

Saturday morning started with a long riverside run.

A shower, hair wash.

Fifty minutes of oboe practice. Gah! A couple of annoying duck squawks. *Round* the *sound. Round* the *sound.* Her new reed was still too tangy—it needed some more breaking in. She knuckle-jiggled her face muscles against her teeth.

An attempt at an art journal entry. *What does it mean? What does it mean to me?* She wrote a response to the sequence in the film *American Beauty* where the boy next door has filmed the plastic bag blowing around in the wind. A mundane object imbued with a balletic beauty. Fragility. Vulnerability. Hmmm. It felt a bit bullshitty, but that was probably okay, given

Ms. Halabi's playground/laboratory instruction. The journal was a place to explore. It was a relief to have a place like that, away from the land of rights and wrongs. *What does it mean to me?*

She created a new page border by repeatedly writing out a quote from Picasso—*Art is a lie that tells the truth*—and filled the page by writing a response to it as it pertained to her work. Little things combining to show us something new, something larger.

She did an image search of footpath and street surveyor marks from around the world, and bookmarked a few images to print at school.

She image-searched some photography of metal surfaces and old glass.

Good to get so much ticked off the list before 11 a.m.

Because *the early bird catches the worm.*

Those old wacko English proverbs and idiomatic sayings were great. It was one of the things she and Debi did when Vân Ước was in year five, in their first year together at homework club. They weren't forms of English she ever heard at home. *It takes one to know one. A tempest in a teacup. A stitch in time saves nine.*

Her mother used occasional mystifying Vietnamese equivalents, like, *If you put in the work to sharpen the steel, it will one day turn into needles. Laugh at others today and tomorrow others will laugh at you.* And others that were simply a variation on study hard: *The hand works, the mouth is allowed to chew. A good beginning is half the battle.*

● ● ●

After a couple more hours of homework, it was time to collect Jess and go to work. Five hours of making rice paper rolls at Henry Ha Minh Rolls on Chapel Street. Seating for twelve only, and the rest was takeaway, the long queue a permanent fixture. The kitchen was as big as the seating area. Six people covered Saturday's prep and rolling. You had to work fast. *Fast and Fresh*: that was the simple sell.

Henry had two other small but equally popular places: Henry Ha Minh Dumplings and Henry Ha Minh Barbecue. He was a hard-line minimalist. One perfect, tiny range at each outlet. His signage was all typeset in lowercase Courier. And each cafe was painted in blackboard paint so walls became a changing artwork/message board for the day. Today, he'd written: *The object of art is to give life a shape…Jean Anouilh*. His girlfriend, Tiên, was an interior designer and as much of a perfectionist and control freak as Henry. When he did the occasional pop-up stall with rolls, buns, and barbecue—Henry Ha Minh Pops Up—social media wet itself with excitement.

She and Jess were a fabulously efficient production line. Vermicelli noodles, finely shredded lettuce, then either chicken, two strands of chives, and two Vietnamese mint leaves, perfectly positioned on a just-overlapping diagonal, or roast duck with hoisin sauce and spring onion, or tiger prawn with julienned green pawpaw and coriander leaves. Roll, roll, roll. Working so hard, with such concentration, even on a menial task, the time went pretty quickly. Vân Ước was surprised when Gary came over and told them to take their break. Vân Ước and Jess had decided long ago that Gary's wardrobe contained nothing but black T-shirts, black jeans, and his signature red bandannas. They could never decide how many he had of each. Cam and Bec, who had been prepping, took over the rolling.

If the weather was fine, she and Jess always went outside for their break. Eyes needed the relaxation of a more distant horizon after looking closely at rice paper rolls, twelve up, for two hours. They were in the alleyway beside the cafe, sitting on the milk crate and cushion seats that were dragged out on the first break of the day and stacked and packed up at closing time. Gary's preferred music of the moment filtered out: Dionne Warwick singing Burt Bacharach songs.

"I love this one," said Jess. It was "Trains and Boats and Planes."

"Me too."

"I think of this album as basically an instruction manual for life."

"Really?" asked Vân Ước, in a vagued-out trance.

"Unless you think that the moment I wake up I say a little prayer for an unspecified other, before I put on my makeup, when you know I don't even wear makeup, no, not really. I was being stupid. For humor."

"I haven't *studied* the lyrics, okay?"

"Yeah, well, they don't really bear examining." Jess opened a bag of Cheezels, her current break snack favorite. "Does it ever occur to you that we should look for other work?"

"How come?"

"We are Vietnamese Australian girls making rice paper rolls."

"So?"

"Well, we haven't exactly spread our cultural wings."

"What do you want to do, flip burgers?"

"Yuck, no, because, smell."

"Work in a shop?"

"Yuck, no, subservience. *Have you found everything you need today? Can I help you with that? It really looks great on you.*"

"Then what?"

"No, I'm happy—I'm just saying, just *noting*, that we're living quite the cliché."

"Suits me. Work's work. Henry's great. And we get food." Vân Ước bit into a prawn roll.

Jess had put a Cheezel on each fingertip and was nibbling them off, one at a time. They were still wearing their paper hygiene hats, so should probably at least have put their backs to the alleyway in case anyone they knew walked by, but Vân Ước felt too work-zonked to care.

"Why do you think it is that I don't like actual cheese, but I love Chee*zels*?" asked Jess.

"Because there's no actual cheese in Cheezels?"

"Though there is the thing called cheese powder," said Jess, looking at the ingredients list on the pack on her knee, nibbling the Cheezel from her left-hand little finger.

A group of girls tumbled across the alleyway, laughing, carrying Henry Ha Minh takeaway bags. One of them was Holly. She spotted Vân Ước and Jess, and pointed. Laughter spurted from the group. Vân Ước froze. She didn't want to give them the satisfaction of looking embarrassed or apologetic.

"Who or what are they?" asked Jess.

"Just girls from school," said Vân Ước.

Another gale of laughter issued from them as they walked off.

"Are they friends of *his*?"

"Yes."

"The case against him just got stronger."

19

Cleaning the apartment with her mother took up a couple of hours every Sunday morning. When her mother was sick, her father took over. The place might not be glamorous, but it was spotless. She didn't think all families would run a damp cloth along every single freaking baseboard every week, for instance. Or have such sparkling plugholes. If only they could get some air through the place, though. The windows didn't open wide, and there was no cross ventilation. Heavy mesh security grilles covered the windows that looked out onto the shared public hallways, and those windows didn't open at all.

She packed her camera after the bleach-fest and went down to take some midday-light photos for her portfolio. In the foyer, she crossed paths with Jess, who was on her way in. They headed outside together, wandering over to their favorite outdoor garden area, the bench under a stand of ghost gums.

"I forgot to ask yesterday—how's your mum going?" said Jess.

"Not great. I'm tablet-counting, though, so I guess she'll feel better one of these days. Where've you been?"

"School. We're doing the toy and book drive."

A pang of school-homesickness hit her. Her old school did a massive toy drive every year to gather, sort, clean up, and distribute toys for asylum-seeker resource centers to send to the detention centers. How relaxing it would be to be back with her old friends and her old teachers. Even after a couple of years, it was still exhausting being in aspiration land at Crowthorne Grammar. "I wish we were little again, sometimes."

"Not me. I'm not doing any more kid time than I have to."

"All that pushing our parents have done. Do you think they get the irony that the more we do what they want, the less we can connect with them?"

"Pushing us to succeed is pushing us out of their gang?"

"Yeah."

"I'm pretty sure my parents don't know what irony is," said Jess.

"And we don't know the Vietnamese word for it."

"I mean, it is irony, isn't it?"

"Yeah, I think that would come under the situational irony umbrella."

"It's kind of sad." Vân Ước opened her camera case and swapped lenses.

"We're transitional."

"Band name? *Transitional Mews*."

"Mmm, an oboe and a violin. I'm not seeing it."

"There are kids not much younger than us whose grandparents came on boats. They're a whole generation in. Parents with proper jobs and perfect English."

"Like we'll be."

"Our kids won't be able to keep us in the dark like we can with our parents." Jess got up and stretched. "I feel kinda sorry for them."

Vân Ước headed for the street as Jess turned back toward the building. "Yeah, well, I feel kinda sorry for us."

● ● ●

Her father had a chicken *phở* on the stove.

Vân Ước emerged, starving, from her bedroom, after a massive load of math homework and an intense "What's with Billy?" wondering session.

Her *ba* smiled at her, gave her a significant look, and pointed at the closed bedroom door.

"Please chop the herbs now," he said.

Vân Ước started cutting up the coriander and Vietnamese mint he had ready on the chopping board. "This smells SO DELICIOUS," she replied loudly, playing along.

"And very healthy food. So good for you."

"Just what you need when you've been feeling sick."

"Now the noodles, and then we can eat."

Her mother opened the bedroom door. She looked tired, but had a small smile on her face. "Why don't you two just come into the bedroom and shout at me while I'm lying down."

"Mama, perfect timing!"

"It does smell good. I'll sit up and eat a little bit."

Watching her father happily draining noodles, arranging the bowls, ladling in stock, Vân Ước felt relieved. Out of bed. Out of the bedroom. Eating. Good signs.

Her father believed his strategy of luring her mother from her bed with tantalizing food smells had worked. And her mother, the most obstinate woman imaginable, let him think it.

20

Vân Ước arrived at the lockers after preschool orchestra practice on Monday morning to find Annie in the middle of a heated dispute with Pippa. She listened idly as she got out her laptop and copy of *Ariel* for first period, English.

"I am too off sugar, you dweeb," Annie said to Pippa.

"But you just put about a gallon of honey in your tea in the common room. I was there right next to you, so...you're not. Off sugar," Pippa said, in her patient, slightly trippy voice. "You're actually mainlining sugar."

"Honey isn't sugar," Annie said, closing her locker with a bang.

"But it's *a* sugar," Pippa said. "It's in the sugar *family*."

"Listen, sugar is white and comes in a bowl, and, it's like

POISON. Honey is a yellow liquid. It's healthy because it's made by bees, who, PS, we would die without, because they pollinate our food."

"No one's saying bees aren't like totally good guys and all, but honey *is* a sugar in dietary terms," said Pippa. "Put it this way: if ants like it, it's a sugar, babe."

Holly walked in with Tiff, and stopped dead when she saw Vân Ước.

"Security alert—lock up your belongings," she said.

"What are you talking about?" asked Annie.

"Didn't you hear? You know that cardigan Vân Ước had on last week? She 'found' it," Holly said, doing the quotation mark fingers in the air. "So, just keep an eye on your valuables."

"Oooh, I loved that cardigan," said Pippa. "Where did you find it?"

"In the Botanic Gardens," said Vân Ước.

"What do you mean—it was just lying around?" said Annie.

"No, I would have left it, if it had been." Finally, an opportunity to tell her story without Holly's false spin on it. She found an extra shred of courage as she saw Michael arrive.

"It had a tag pinned to it that said..." Of course, she remembered—she had proof. She opened her locker again. "I've still got it here...somewhere." She pulled out her backpack and felt around inside the front pocket where she'd put it. "It *was* here. I must have lost it."

"How convenient," said Holly.

"I haven't done anything wrong. I found the cardigan, and I know what the tag said..."

"And I know a liar when I see one." Holly ostentatiously locked her locker. "But do let us know if you find this nonexistent tag." She gave Vân Ước an unpleasant Cheshire Cat smile.

If all the world hated you, and believed you wicked, while your own conscience approved you, and absolved you from guilt, you would not be without friends. Huh! Cold comfort. Of course that was the saintly Helen Burns speaking, not Jane Eyre. Jane's rejoinder had been, *No; I know I should think well of myself; but that is not enough: if others don't love me I would rather die than live—I cannot bear to be solitary and hated, Helen.* Jane was always spot on the money. Who wanted to be solitary and hated? Who didn't want to be popular and loved?

● ● ●

Ms. Norton, who was also another class's homeroom teacher, was running a few minutes late for English, and the whole room was humming with chat when Billy arrived. He came over to Vân Ước. "I've been scouted by Brown," he said. "They want me and Ben to row for them." Vân Ước could see Billy's friends exchanging looks: a few aberrations were becoming a pattern—what was Billy doing talking to that girl *again*? With his full focus on her, she was unable to ignore him.

"Brown. You mean … Ivy League Brown?" she said.

"Yep." And as though struck by an important realization, he added, "They have great art schools there, too." She wasn't the only one giving him the shock bomb. What he seemed to be saying was that she, too, might like to study in America.

124

Holly looked at her with open hostility. But Ben made light of it. "Actually, they have a whole lot of good universities there. And Robbo says we'll get more offers. Now we just have to ace the regatta this weekend."

"I think we'll be okay. I pulled a 6:26 this morning," said Billy.

Vân Ước saw a quickly covered spark of annoyance cross Ben's face. Billy was talking about his ergo time. Six minutes, twenty-six seconds. She wondered what his splits were.

Ms. Norton came in with apologies, making sure that everyone had completed their practice session by now, or had them scheduled for some time that week and had made appointments with her for their first orals.

Vân Ước and Billy were meeting after school on Wednesday. She knew for sure if she looked up he'd be looking at her. She managed not to look up.

21

On Wednesday, straight after her oboe class and his training session were finished Vân Ước found herself leaving school with Billy Gardiner. She was side by side on a footpath with him. Billy Gardiner. On her way to his house. To Billy Gardiner's house. She knew from the class contact lists that he lived within walking distance of the school. He'd showered after gym and his hair was still dripping, soaking his shirt. He smelled great. Looked great. She tried not to look, not to smell.

She had told her parents she'd be at a compulsory after-school English session. Her mother didn't even bother asking to see the letter from school. She must have figured out years ago that her daughter was reliable to a boring degree. The benefit of all those years of perfect behavior was that she had a fair amount of freedom in daylight hours, though rarely anything to squander it on. She smiled. She was acting as though this actually constituted a transgressive activity, when what she was doing was walking to a real, compulsory after-school English study session. What a loser she was. Even when she was breaking free, she wasn't.

Billy looked at her. "It's the *secret smile*. The Vân Ước special."

She immediately replaced the smile with a neutral expression. He couldn't possibly interpret that any particular way. She thought of Mr. Rochester studying Jane Eyre's expressions: *There was much sense in your smile: it was very shrewd...*

"It's the *Vân Ước is giving nothing away* face," he said. "I like that I get the faces to myself for once. Now I can ask you what you're thinking."

"You've had since year nine to ask what I'm thinking. You took your own good time."

"You came in year nine?"

"Yup."

"Huh. Who knew?"

He looked genuinely puzzled, and fleetingly unsure of himself, as he should, because wasn't he really asking the question, *Why am I suddenly* fascinated *by someone I never noticed before, even though she's been in my class for two years?*

He was unlikely to be speculating that his feelings might be nothing more than wish-induced hokum.

But she was.

Billy was quiet for a stretch of at least two minutes— unusual—before they turned into his street, which ran into a road that flanked one boundary of the Botanic Gardens. They stopped at a high brick wall covered in well-trimmed ficus. He unlocked a tall wrought-iron gate decorated with leaves and flowers and ushered her into his world.

● ● ●

On a sideboard crammed with photos of, she guessed, family and extended family and friends, in a forest of silver frames, there was one photo to which she was particularly drawn. Billy's parents, presumably—a wedding-day shot. Straight blonde hair, a simple, collarbone-exposing neckline, thick fabric that stood a little way from the skin, casting a soft shadow. Eye-shining laughter, champagne flutes raised, a toast. The large square diamond. It could be a Tiffany ad. It could not be a more stark contrast to her own family.

She thought, inevitably, of something—not the worst thing, no, not by far—on the list of things she'd never dared to ask her father. On boats, in cases such as her parents', when people sat crammed together like livestock, becalmed and dying, it wasn't uncommon that they would resort to drinking their own urine, or giving sips of urine to their children, desperate to keep them hydrated. She'd dipped the tip of her little finger into a sample she had to produce at the doctor's one day, when she was thirteen. It tasted funky and made her gag. Mouthfuls? No. No way. She would have perished, a weakling.

The sense of excess here flooded her senses. Space! The entry hall was bigger than her living/dining and kitchen area combined. One wall featured a gallery-huge piece of indigenous art. The entrance lobby of her apartment building featured unpainted redbrick walls, a line of missing tiles on the floor right outside the elevators, and a sign that said, NO SPITTING OR HAWKING. FINE $300 in three languages.

The stuff of which things were made! Curtains in the sitting room fell to sit heavily on the floor, slightly overlong. Windowsills were deep enough to sit on. She thought of Jane Eyre's reading nook. In the library, the windows had solid wooden folding shutters, painted white. The books! They lived here—never had to be returned to a public library. The rug felt densely woven, thick and soft underfoot. Here was a sense of air and light, an environment controlled. Nothing intruded. Nothing unwelcome could find its way in. No cooking smells invaded this area. It had its own lovely smells: the glass vase of flowers, as big as a bucket; a hint of furniture polish, beeswax. But it smelled most of all like...cleanness, and fresh air.

Where she lived, there were pockets that would forever hold the ghosts of a thousand *phở*s. A lack of proper ventilation meant that their apartment held the heat for too long on summer days like this.

The walls here must be so thick. This room was quiet, and cool, despite the breathless heat outside. Maybe there were other people in the house, maybe not. You'd never know.

At her place, every conversation could be heard from anywhere in the apartment. Bathroom noises were all unavoidably shared. And, coming in from either side, neighbors' phone calls, music, arguments, plumbing noises, and TV were constant visitors.

Here, she felt like a flower finally in its right environment, her petals opening one by one to absorb the beauty, and then folding back up to protect herself from the fact that this was not her world.

She knew of people who lived like this, from magazines, but seeing at close range the vast span of difference between her life and Billy's almost made her laugh with disbelief at the unfairness of it all. Who had decided that some should have so little and others so much?

She hoped none of this was visible on her face, especially the bit about tasting her own pee.

She turned to Billy. "What are these? It's such a pretty scent." She bent to sniff the big-headed yellow blooms made up of many small flowers threaded with delicate red stamens.

"Yeah, they're ginger flowers, I think—my mum likes them, too."

Billy leaned in, smiling. What? Was he going to kiss her? She heard a confused rushing in her ears, and felt a tug of desire so strong it was like being winded. She held the table edge behind her for balance. But he just brushed the tip of her nose softly with his little finger and said, "Pollen." He stayed close, looking into her eyes. Whatever else might have been about to happen didn't, because she sneezed five times in quick succession and had to fish a tissue from her pocket and blow her nose.

Classic mood-breaker.

She gave herself a stern mental shake: nothing was going to

happen except her fantasy intruding into reality, an uninvited guest.

"Does she—does your mum arrange the flowers?"

"Usually. I think. If she's around. Let's grab something to eat and go to my room."

She didn't want to leave the beauty of this space, but managed a few muted tap-dance steps to relieve her feelings as she followed Billy.

The kitchen was another revelation. It looked like a glamorous laboratory. Perfect white tiles, stainless steel, and a woman wearing an apron emerging from a doorway. Vân Ước froze. Meet the parents? She wasn't ready for that.

"Mel, this is Vân Ước. Vân Ước, Mel."

"Lovely to meet you." Mel expertly jostled and slid the contents of the large baking tray she was carrying onto two cooling racks sitting ready on the kitchen bench. The oven must have its own room. "Cheese-and-chive scones—help yourselves. And those peaches are ripe." She nodded at the huge fruit bowl, which like everything around here looked like a prop in a design magazine.

"Thanks, Mel," said Billy, loading up a plate. "How was your day?"

Who was this Mel?

"It was wonderful, thank you, William. And if by *How was your day?* you mean *What's for dinner?*, it's a Malaysian chicken curry with jasmine rice, fresh mango and mint chutney, and steamed broccolini. And I'm making a lemon delicious, but with limes."

Billy smiled his wide smile. He looked like the handsome man in the wedding photo, with the champagne, but scruffy. "You are my hero," he said.

Mel pretended to be impervious to Billy's charm, but Vân Ước could see that she liked him a lot. "I know it. Don't let him eat it all," she said to Vân Ước with a brisk, friendly smile.

Vân Ước didn't know who she was, and didn't know what to say. The old dudes did, though. *Look at her/She's pressed the mute button again/Smiling, yes/But does she expect people to read her mind?/Apparently/Winning tactic.*

* * *

Vân Ước followed Billy up the stairs, a view to the deep garden from the landing, along a corridor, and into his room. "Who's Mel?" she asked.

"Our house manager."

"What does she do?"

"She runs the place. The parentals both work and they like things to run smoothly when they're away. And when they're here. They're both pretty much control freaks." He saw the momentary look of panic on her face. "And don't worry, they're away till next week."

"So, she...cooks? Cleans?"

"No, we've got cleaners. She cooks. She shops. She pays bills, coordinates other staff, like cleaners and gardeners, supervises homework—well, she used to—and does any picking up and dropping off of us kids when we need it...I mean, my sister's not here, she's at university now—I don't know, shit like that. She gets everything organized. She's lived with us since I was five."

Billy was gazing at her again.

"Okay, well, let's get on with it," she said in a matter-of-fact tone that she hoped concealed how overwhelming she found him and his world.

"Scone?" he asked, backing into his bedroom, holding the tray. The room was huge, on the northeast corner of the house. There was a double bed, drum kit, windows on two walls, sofa, cluttered desk, over which was a corkboard with a montage of photos—a few she could see were of crew members, including Billy, standing side by side, huge grins, index fingers thrust upward in triumph, holding up medals, expansive bookshelves...and no visible pile of dirty laundry, despite all the training gear he must go through every day.

She took a scone, and bit into it. Oh, god. It was an explosion of great flavor, light, cheesy, flaky, with fresh basil as well as chives. "Wow. You realize you live in the land of Take What You Want?"

He laughed. "I know. Mel is, like, the best."

Vân Uớc sat at Billy's desk, and he sat on a comfortable-looking chair that he pulled close. They opened their laptops.

"Let's look at the session transcripts first, so we know what we're supposed to be doing," she said. She'd already read them the night before, but she was prepared to go through the motions of being a regular, non-obsessive workaholic student.

This meant that she was at liberty to watch Billy as he read.

He tucked a strand of hair behind his ear. She could see he was skimming and not particularly interested.

"Poetry. It's, like, there's only so much you can say about so few words. Am I right?" He glanced up. "Sorry, I'm wrecked from training. I'd rather sit here and continue through the catalog of the Vân Uớc facial expressions collection."

"You'll see pissed off soon, if I end up doing all the work."

"Woohoo! The feisty face."

She ignored him. Billy Gardiner might be Billy Gardiner, but nobody was going to stop her doing the work. "I think one of the things we are expected to do—if we look at this—is to help shape the discussion. We're not just answering questions."

Billy looked at his computer glumly. "Yeah. Okay, let's go through and highlight some more of the requirements, and then we'll talk about the text?"

"Deal."

"So, there's also this thing—some allusion to criticism, and some personal responses." He looked up. "Do you have personal responses?"

"I love Plath," she said. "I have more responses than they'll want. I just don't like talking." Oops. She'd said it.

"Uh-huh," Billy said. "I've noticed that. How come?"

"Shy, I guess."

"I don't like talking in class, either."

She couldn't help laughing. That was absurd. He did nothing *but* talk in class.

"I mean, I can't be fucked talking about the work. But I know—I know this is the year to knuckle down."

"You've managed without any knuckling so far?"

"Yeah, but my parents will kill me if I don't get serious about studying this year." He sighed. "I've kind of been dreading it, to be honest. This is officially the end of fun times."

He looked grave, a look so uncharacteristic that she had to ask, "Why the pressure? You do okay, don't you?" She had him placed in the top 10 percent, top 2–3 percent if he bothered working, but she didn't want him knowing she'd watched that closely. He was a brainy slacker.

"I need better than okay to get into medicine. I'll be a fourth-generation doctor. I have a *contribution* to make! Supporting Panadol sales when I'm hungover isn't enough."

She was dying to blurt out: *Me too me too me too, my parents want me to study medicine, too.* "Is that a problem? You don't want to be a doctor?"

"I don't know. Probably not. Who knows? I don't know what I want for breakfast tomorrow. Okay, that's a lie—I mean, I eat the same shit every morning—but, you know, *no*. I don't have a fucking life plan. Jesus, I'm seventeen." He shut his laptop. "Sorry. You don't swear much, do you?"

"Not particularly." Not out loud.

"Is that like a religious thing? A...Buddhist thing, or whatever?"

"I wouldn't really know. My family's Catholic."

Billy had the grace to look embarrassed. "Sorry. Jeez, I'm a klutz. I haven't even asked you stuff like that."

"It's fine. We don't really know each other."

"But after we share our innermost thoughts on 'Daddy' and

'Tulips' we're gonna. Am I right?" That smile contained something addictive. The snack equivalent of his smile was cheese Doritos. You always wanted one more.

"We'll know what we each think about 'Daddy' and 'Tulips,' which I guess is a start."

● ● ●

After an hour of being lost in the complicated beauty and anger of "Daddy," Vân Ước stretched and stood up.

"No!" Billy said. "We're just getting warmed up."

"But I've got to get going. My parents are expecting me home by dinnertime."

"Have dinner here—there'll be heaps."

"Sorry, I can't."

"Can I walk you home?"

"No! Thanks."

Billy looked crestfallen. "Are you coming to the regatta on Saturday?"

"No."

"Please come—you can see me row."

It was amazing seeing the whole Billy Gardiner unlimited-confidence phenomenon up close. Who in the world assumed that the rest of the world was ready and waiting to watch them, love them?

"Oh no. The *I'm unimpressed* face. I guess that does sound arrogant."

"I work Saturdays, anyway. Even if I were the fan-girl type, I couldn't come."

"I was thinking more 'Go, school' than fan girl, but fair enough. Have a peach before you go?"

She shook her head. Peaches were not something she would venture to eat in public. One more inhibition of the kid from another planet. She dreaded being inadvertently loud, messy, or unmannerly. She'd seen a table of whities looking askance at her own family happily slurping up bowls of noodles once, and had never quite got over the disapproval you could innocently attract just by eating your dinner.

Billy had no such qualms. He took a huge, dripping bite and wiped juice off his chin with the back of his hand. "Oh, man, that's seriously good. You don't know what you're missing out on."

Vân Ước looked at him, here, in his lush habitat. He was so wrong, she thought as she left his bedroom; she knew exactly what she was missing out on.

22

It went like this: Make sure the tablets get taken. Be patient. Be nice. Shop. Help with dinner. And in a few weeks things should improve, recalibrate. She was so used to the annual slump, she was almost taking it in stride, even though this year wasn't shaping up as the big improvement she'd hoped for. They'd had a wobbly start, but having a proper diagnosis and a plan meant there was hope on the horizon. And her mother was sticking with the group therapy, still going, ten weeks in, a big win.

"What did you talk about tonight?"

"Things you children don't need to know."

"Like what?"

"I gave them my *bánh chưng* recipe." She shrugged. "They know mine's the best. Some of them just buy it."

Vân Ước knew when she was being diverted with talk of New Year's rice cake recipes, but she didn't mind tonight. Her mother seemed in slightly better spirits.

"Brush your hair, Mama?"

Her mother nodded, and sat down on a kitchen chair. Vân Ước went into her parents' bedroom, breathing in its mingled slightly peppery and warm camphor smell, the ever-present ghosts of her mother's perfume and the Tiger Balm ointment her father rubbed into his finger joints to soothe the aching, and got the hairbrush.

She paused at the wardrobe mirror. When she was very little, two people used to stand beside her reflection in the mirror: a boy and an old lady. They felt like a benign presence. She'd never told anyone about them, not even Jess, and she stopped seeing them when she was still young, about four—before she started school, anyway. For a while she had pushed her face into the mirror, trying to see them somewhere, at the most distant angle, deep in the speckled reflection, but they never showed themselves again. Now they felt like something she must surely have imagined, though part of her still believed in them.

She stood behind her mother's chair and brushed her hair gently for about five minutes, drawing the brush smoothly from forehead to nape, over and over, in the way her mother liked. It was the only sustained physical contact she seemed to enjoy. Her usual mode of a kiss good-bye, for instance, was the kiss-and-push-on-your-way. She wasn't a snuggler. No surprise, really, that this acceptable affection came via a prickly implement.

An envelope with the school crest on it was on the bench. Already opened. That meant Jess's mum must have been in today. Her English wasn't as bad as Vân Ước's mother's, and she sometimes read a letter for her if Vân Ước wasn't around.

"What's the note from school?"

"A night meeting for information about art. Next week."

"Oh, right. You don't have to go to those things. I can pass on anything important."

"This one your *ba* wants to go to. We want to make sure there's no more art for next year. It wastes so much of your time. You need to study only sciences and math for medicine. Everyone knows that."

Vân Ước took a calming breath. Whatever happened she had to be allowed to continue with her art. Unfortunately, this early in the term, it wasn't too late for her to change subjects if her parents made a big enough fuss and the school listened. If her parents, for instance, told the school that Vân Ước had implied that art was just for this year alone, and not a two-year course, which it was, she could be in trouble.

An even worse scenario would be if her parents went to the information night and met Ms. Halabi and she gave them the big encouragement-talk about how Vân Ước's portfolio plans looked good, and she could be confident about aiming for art school—something that normal parents might be thrilled to hear.

"They don't expect scholarship parents to attend, Ma. And they don't like scholarship parents telling them what they should do. I told you: They want us to take a wide range of subjects. Not just science. That's what IB is all about. If you complain about art, they will think you don't understand the IB."

Ack. She felt awful pulling the *scholarship parents* line. She'd used it before. She kind of relied on it.

She knew it was cheating to soothe her conscience with the fact that her mother didn't need any extra stress just now, but she always came to a dead end when she imagined how to breach the gap between her parents' land of study hard, make money, be eternally secure, and her dream destination: artist, probable low income, no security. So, for now she had to keep a handle on the information flow.

When her father returned home after his game of cards, and her mother was safely in bed, Vân Ước decided, again, to try to find out some "things you children don't need to know."

"*Ba*, we read at school that Vietnamese refugees from when you and Mama came over were mostly 'economic' refugees. Is that right?" Not strictly a lie, because she had read it in the school library, but a mention of school in the question might mean her father would be more willing to talk.

Her father looked at her for the longest time, as though deciding whether to talk, what to say.

"If they mean the war was over, that's right," he began. "But things were very bad. Your grandfather had served in the army; he was in a reeducation camp. Everything we owned was confiscated. I was put in jail for no reason, for being 'a person of suspicion.' We had no future there. No life at all. But, yes, I suppose if they say it, we were economic refugees." He shrugged. "The communists certainly took away any chance of making a living."

"Can I ask you about how you got out? The boat trip?"

"Is this also for school?" He was obviously becoming impatient, and she took her cue to back off.

"No, *ba*, just me wanting to know."

"We made it. We got here. Now don't go upsetting Mama with your questions. She's told you she doesn't like to speak about it."

"But why?"

"It was hard for her. Now no more questions! Time for some study, or sleep."

23

The next morning, as she left home early to be on time for baroque ensemble practice at school, Vân Ước tried to stop wondering about her father's words, *It was hard for her,* and took a moment to breathe in the cool morning of what would be a melting-hot day. The sun shining at a low angle through the deserted playground, the damp grass, the stand of gum trees that, if she framed her eye line just the right way, could make her feel that she was back at Mount Fairweather.

Matthew, setting out for a run, minus beret, whipped past her, giving her braid a playful flick, a habit that had riled her seriously in primary school and still did, in a watered-down way.

"Hey, wait," she called.

"What's up?"

"What's with Nick? Why's he being such an idiot?"

"Code of the bros. Can't talk."

Vân Ước rolled her eyes.

"Yeah, okay, I know. He's doing nangs and pills and not much schoolwork."

"Have you said anything?"

"I've said stuff, but he's not listening. He's pretty much hanging with River and those dudes now."

"God."

"Yeah." Matthew shot her a *but what are you gonna do about it?* look, and ran off.

As she walked out the gates, she was distracted; no one liked seeing someone they'd known since little-kid days take a turn for the stupid.

She looked down, focusing on one of her silver disks embedded in the footpath. She had just squatted down to examine it, hoping there would be some unclouded morning light for photography this weekend so she could get a shiny, east-side-lit image, when a large shadow created an annoying obstruction. She looked up. If she were ever to swear aloud, this was a classic *WTF* moment.

"Why, Billy? *Why* are you here?"

"Walk you to school?"

She stood up and stalked past him, angry.

He caught up, trying to relieve her of her turtlelike backpack. She yanked it away and tried to walk faster than him. Not easy. He was a boy with a long stride. She looked back at the apartments anxiously. Someone would be seeing this, for sure.

"How did you even know what time I'd be leaving home?"

"You've got baroque ensemble rehearsal."

She stopped and turned to face him. "Let's recap..."

"It's *not* baroque ensemble rehearsal?"

She pinned those baby blues with her most penetrating look. "Just yesterday, you acknowledged that you didn't know I came to Crowthorne Grammar in year nine?"

"Yeah..."

"So, I was there, but you couldn't see me...or you didn't notice I was there."

"I guess."

"Last term we were both at Mount Fairweather—could you even tell me what house I was in?"

Billy looked at the sky. "Nope."

"It was Reynolds. So, close quarters for a whole term, only one-quarter of the year level there, and you couldn't have located me if you needed to. And yet now—out of the blue—you're virtually stalking me."

"I wouldn't use that word."

"Last week you followed me into the *girls' bathroom*, Billy. What would you think if you were me? Honest answer."

"I'd be thinking, *Can this be a mortal, or is it a god of rowing, recently scouted by Brown, walking next to me, trying to carry my backpack against my will?*"

"That is pretty much on the money, if you replace *god* with *stalker*," she said.

Hmmm, *stalker of rowing*, majorly dumb comeback. Luckily, he didn't seem to notice.

She was a patient girl, someone with all too much practice at delaying gratification, but she was getting really sick of not knowing what was going on.

"Given this agreed-upon reversal from complete lack of awareness of my existence formerly to annoying overfocus on me now, would you agree it's reasonable for me to wonder why?"

Unless he was a great actor, and she'd seen no evidence of that to date, Billy was surprised at her vehemence.

"I don't get why it's a problem."

Was it possible that someone could go through life assuming the whole world loved him? Expecting to be welcome wherever he happened to turn up?

"Our class does a group double take when you speak to me. Haven't you noticed that people are a little surprised? Why are you speaking to me? Following me around at school? Coming to my place at dawn?"

"I don't know. I really liked hanging with you last night."

"That was homework, not hanging."

"It was a homework hang."

She couldn't help smiling. This was, after all, her number one mew boy, giving a very good impression of bending over backward to be nice to her.

"And we had *food*. That really takes it from homework to a hang in my book," he said confidently. Because, of course, his book would be *the* book.

They walked on. She would have given a great deal at this moment to spend sixty seconds inside his brain.

"If you're smiling, does that mean I can hold your hand?"

She reapplied the frown. They were walking along Albert Street, her usual route to school, where there were countless people who might report back to her mother by lunchtime today at the latest; despite the fact the street was almost deserted at this hour, she knew the windows had eyes.

"No!"

She stopped and turned to face him. "Just tell me what changed."

"What what?"

"Exactly when did I go from being invisible to being visible?"

This was his cue to say that he'd gradually been noticing her over the last year or so—he hadn't wanted to be obvious in his attentions, but he knew by now that, though quiet, she was smart; though shy, she had a sense of humor; though not a self-promoter, she was a dedicated, passionate artist . . .

Billy smiled. "It was that class—the first week back, when the visiting writer came. The one with the pink hair?"

Vân Ước stopped dead. It took a huge effort to retain her cool, but she managed it. Just. "Yep. Yep, I remember. So, what was it that made you notice me?"

Billy nodded and looked into the middle distance as though he were trying to replay the scene in his mind. He looked puzzled. "It was like you suddenly had a spotlight on you."

"So, just to be clear: it was a sudden thing more than a gradual thing."

"Can't answer that—because who knows what's been going on subliminally and for how long? Am I right?"

God, of all the annoying times for him to become reflective. "Billy, just concentrate on that particular class—what else did you notice about me, if anything?"

"The best way to put it, I guess, is that it was just blindingly obvious that you were the most interesting person in the room." Billy smiled the addictive smile. "Apart from me."

She felt sick to the pit of her stomach. She had to force herself to breathe in to avoid a footpath vomit. She needed to sit down, fast, and put her head between her legs.

It was like being pulled apart with no chance of reconnecting the two halves again. Wasn't this proof that her most ridiculous, improbable fantasy was being delivered to her on a plate? But how could she—*she could not*—believe in the means by which the fantasy appeared to have been delivered? A little glass vial? A wish being granted? This was not a phenomenon of the real world. She knew it as well as she knew her own name.

Her name, Cloudwish—could that have anything to do with anything? Of course not! Things inside her head were hectic and preposterous.

A tram stop seat saved her from falling in a heap. "*Shazbat*," she said as she sat down, slipped out of her backpack straps, and dropped her head between her knees.

"What the fuck's a shazbat?" Billy asked fondly. "Are you okay? Did you have breakfast?"

She lifted her head. "*Shazbat* is an alien swear word from an antique American sitcom called *Mork and Mindy* that Jess's parents got in a DVD collection of old TV shows. I'm fine. I had a humongous breakfast." She dropped her head again. Circulation normalized. Reengaging with her backpack, she stood up.

"Are you really okay?" Billy asked, touching her shoulder gently.

"Yup," she said, and risked giving him her first unguarded smile. She had to figure all of this out, but, hell, why not enjoy the aberration while it lasted?

Billy appeared to be appropriately dazzled, and she widened her smile in response.

Bizarro world, I'm moving in, she thought. Who knew for how long?

24

Before she and Billy parted company, he to the gym, she to rehearsal with Polly, who played cello, he said, "I've got a little plan to mess with the collective minds of the staff."

"What sort of plan?"

"It involves a bit of photography."

"I'm on a scholarship. I have to behave myself."

"Don't worry. I'm the perp. I'll do the time. I just need someone with a good camera to direct me."

"It's a likely no, but talk to me later."

"Are you going to watch Miro at lunchtime?"

She generally preferred to spend lunchtimes reading, but since Lou was Miro's lead singer, she had planned to make an exception. "Yep."

"I'll catch you there."

Polly looked at her, wide-eyed, as Billy gave Vân Ước's hand a good-bye squeeze and left. "Since when has that happened?"

Vân Ước shrugged. "I know." She shook her head, no less mystified than Polly.

• • •

Unraveling knots in the Handel grand concerto—in G minor for two oboes, two violins, cello strings, and continuo, the focus of their rehearsal—was a welcome break from the strange new world of Billy-likes-Vân Ước.

As soon as they finished, as she stretched her neck, wiped her oboe, pulled it apart, and packed it inside its case, she felt the weird new excitement bubbling up in her chest. How was this going to play out? What would the limitations on her new-found charm be? Was there an expiry date? She couldn't even revisit *how the hell was this happening?* It was too much to get her head around. It did not bear scrutiny.

Now that Billy had pinpointed the exact moment of noticing her, his sudden fascination could logically come down to one of two things. Either her wish had come true, or jumping up and down in front of someone you liked could create an instant attraction where none had existed before. Neither scenario seemed remotely plausible.

She was honest enough to admit to herself that in planning to enjoy this, at least for a little while, and going with the wish theory, she was saying yes to living a probable big fat lie: Billy was being duped. For once the joke would be on him. It was simply too tempting, and too intriguing an experience to forgo. But she had the horrible feeling that this would be akin to her childhood habit of saying yes to the giddy thrill of the playground whizz-around, despite knowing for sure that afterward she'd feel sick, stagger, and fall.

● ● ●

At lunchtime she headed for a spot under a shady tree to watch the year-eleven band, Miro, who were just finishing their sound check for the lunchtime concert. She couldn't see Billy yet, so that gave her a chance to experiment. Would he find her and come to her?

"Taken," said Tiff coldly as she was about to sit down, not even very close. "Sorry. We're saving spots." It was amazing the way these girls managed to say "sorry" in a tone that so clearly meant "piss off."

She went to the next tree over and sat alone. From the stage, which was just an elevated paved area at the north edge of the quad, Lou gave her a little wave, and she waved back. A knot of tall boys emerged from the Kessler wing and mooched toward the trees. They stopped near where Tiff had saved space. A couple of them sat down, but Vân Ước saw Billy looking around. He smiled when he saw her and headed straight over, throwing himself down next to her. At least six sets of eyes from the next tree along stared in disbelief and frank hostility. She knew exactly what they were thinking. *He's our friend. What is* our friend *doing with her?*

She let herself have a moment of triumph, looking back at them. *Taken. Yeah, that's right, me, I've taken Billy. From you. He's choosing me.* This was like being in a formula that was being chemically altered. The next thing Vân Ước saw was Sibylla virtually dragging Michael, with whom she'd been sitting on a bench, over to her.

"Hi," Sibylla said, glaring at Billy. She sat herself down between Vân Ước and Billy, a squeezy small space to settle in, and left Michael standing, looking uncomfortable and bemused.

"Dude," said Billy. "Are you going to sit? You're kinda blocking my view." Michael sat down hastily and started opening his package of sandwiches.

Miro was playing their warm-up-the-audience opening number, something thrashy. Vân Ước was grateful for the musical distraction.

Billy was looking at her with regret—their brief time together intruded on. Sibylla was giving her a significant look: *I've got your back, sister.*

And Michael decided now was as good a time as any to ask her a detailed question about their calculus assignment. They had to have the exchange at high volume because of the music.

Sibylla shushed them, saying, "Would you listen to Lou? She's amazing."

The four of them sat, eating lunch and listening, for the

next three songs. Any time Vân Ước glanced toward Billy he was looking at her. Sibylla, in turn, was looking suspiciously at Billy looking at Vân Ước. She'd have to tell Sibylla and Lou that the landscape had changed. What would they make of it? She barely believed it herself. Plus, she didn't really know what "it" was.

The band ended the set with a cover of the Vance Joy song that had been everywhere a couple of years earlier. Their version had a bit more of a trance vibe than the original, and Lou's melodic, wide-ranging voice suited the song beautifully. She sang the line about a girl running down to the riptide. Vân Ước let herself lie back on the grass, plant herself into the heart of the song, and be that girl, the girl who inspired dreamy lines in pretty songs.

Just as Billy was her fantasy real boy, the lead singer of that band was her fantasy celebrity. She hated the official clip for the song that featured a clichéd victim-smudged-makeup woman, but she'd watched a live version on YouTube until she knew it by heart. She knew the water bottles, the little furry monkey, the Howard Arkley portrait of Nick Cave.

She imagined herself in that student house—it didn't matter if it was real, or if an art director had dressed a set: it was real to her. She'd hung out in that room, at dim parties with good loud music that made the neighbors shout over the fence, and fairy lights strung on the walls merging through open windows with the stars strung across the sky, and people not caring, and caring too much, and drinking cheap wine, and breathless kisses in dark hallways.

She loved Vance Joy's voice. It gave her goose bumps. One day she might even get to see the band live. Meanwhile, she'd enjoy those parties—as an artist, she fit right in—in that room in her imagination.

She was still in a delicious half doze when Billy got up, stretched, and said, "Party's at mine on Saturday, after the regatta. Welcome, any friends of Vân Ước's…et cetera." He was looking at Sibylla and Michael.

Vân Ước took his outstretched hand and stood up.

"Only, Holly will probably be there…" he added, looking at Sibylla.

"Who?" Sib asked coldly.

"Come if you want to. I guess if you can avoid each other at school, you can probably manage it at my place, too."

"You'll come, won't you?" Billy said to Vân Ước. "I know you can't make the regatta, but you're not working at night, are you?"

"I don't know if I'd be allowed," said Vân Ước.

"I'll be there," said Sibylla, looking Billy in the eye with a mildly threatening manner. "If Vân Ước goes, I won't be far away."

"Go-od," said Billy, apparently unsure what he'd done to deserve such stern looks from Sibylla.

It was lovely that Sibylla was prepared to protect her at Billy's party, particularly because it would involve social contact with Sibylla's former best friend and now, surely, her least favorite person in the world, Holly.

"Whatever's going on, I will see it," Sibylla added.

"Cool," said Billy, understandably a bit confused by Sibylla's intensity.

As the bell for the end of lunch blared, Billy whispered into Vân Ước's ear, which gave her an unexpected little shudder of pleasure, "Meet me in the common room after last period."

25

The afternoon of calculus seemed to last for about a week. Vân Ước popped into the girls' bathroom adjacent to the lockers for a quick mirror check before heading to the common room. She arrived a few seconds before Billy, relieved to see only a few stragglers collecting things left from earlier in the day or killing time before being picked up.

Billy came in and swept them out. "That's all, folks, thanks for coming, see you tomorrow—show's over, room's taken."

She was intrigued by the willingness of people to do as Billy told them. No one protested or even showed any resentment; they accepted the alpha presence doing what he did best: getting his way. Leading.

She recognized a notebook jammed between two cushions

on the corduroy-covered sofa as Michael's, and picked it up. He was a great absentminded leaver of stuff.

When everyone was shooed away, she expected that Billy might turn to her and throw his arms around her, and the whole soft-focus, swelling orchestral score would happen.

But he had something else in mind. "Have you got your camera?"

She was never without it, just one of the reasons her backpack was always so heavy. As she dug it out, Billy flicked through his phone's photos and showed her a series of images.

It was the security office's panel of CCTV screens. Quite modest, just four screens that rotated through images from the various cameras positioned around the school. Two screens were for interiors, and two for exterior views.

"You and I are going to shoot this room, from that angle"— he pointed at the image of the common room—"And make a print we can stick up there, in front of the camera."

"So it looks like the common room is always empty?"

"Yeah, stop them spying on us, and get our privacy back."

Vân Ước couldn't help smiling. "*I* can't do it. If I get caught I'm in huge trouble. Scholarship students *must demonstrate exemplary behavior at all times.*"

"Like I said, I'll take the blame."

Now he kissed her. Now, when she was unprepared and unguarded, he leaned forward and kissed her gently, and it felt like a question she'd been waiting to hear for the longest time. She opened her lips and her mouth to his, touched one hand to the side of his face, and wondered how it would be possible to live another day in the world that didn't include kissing Billy.

He broke away from the kiss, hands still holding her upper arms, took a deep breath, and exhaled shakily. He leaned down, touching his forehead to hers. "Wow. I wasn't going to do that till Saturday night," he said.

"You had a kiss plan?" she asked, breathless, amazed that words still tumbled out in order following the reinvention of the world.

"Of course I did. It's the only reason I asked my parents if I can have people over on Saturday."

"I'm still not sure if I can come…" she said, falling into the gulf between what his parents might see as normal, acceptable behavior, and what her parents might see as normal, acceptable behavior.

She felt tired and defeated in advance at the acrobatics in reasoning and the half lies that she would have to tell in order to reassure/deceive her parents into allowing her to go out just for one night. "I don't like my chances for the party. But I guess I can help with this."

Based on the image on Billy's phone, it was obvious that it needed to be shot from the security camera's POV with a long depth of field, sharp focus, and tonal clarity. Simple.

Billy had brought in a tall ladder from the cleaners' cupboard in the hallway outside.

She set the camera for him. He climbed up, photographed the room, with their bags out of shot, and climbed down for her to check it. A couple more attempts and he had the angle and focus looking right.

"So long as no one was looking at the screen when you took the photo, you're all sorted. I'll send it to you tonight." She packed her camera away, tucked Michael's notebook in after it, slung her backpack on her shoulders, and said, "I think you're late for training."

"Shit." He folded the ladder and headed out with it, kissing the tips of her fingers as he left.

Michael hurried in, frowning as he crossed paths with Billy. Seeing Vân Ước alone in the common room, his frown deepened. She could swear he knew about the kiss and the rule-breaking.

"This?" she asked, pulling his notebook from her pack.

"Thanks." Michael's momentary relief at having his note-book back didn't distract him from a speech he obviously had prepared.

"It's none of my business—what I'm about to say—but I have decided to say it anyway."

"You're wondering what's going on with me and Billy?"

"I can see that he conforms to a general consensus of what constitutes 'handsome,' and he's undoubtedly one of the most popular guys in the year, for what that's worth..."

"But..."

Michael looked at her—his kindness and generosity at speaking out when they really didn't have that sort of friend-ship made her eyes prickle with tears.

"You know the *but*: he's a self-centered idiot. And I can't see a happy ending if someone like you gets involved with him."

"Like me—how?"

"Someone smart. Someone not of his world. Someone lacking the essential superficiality of his preferred companions." Michael smiled apologetically. "If you can forgive the cliché: I'd hate to see you get hurt."

Here's where Jane might boldly have defended her choice of a partner, pointing out that while the world thought one thing about him, she saw another side to his character. But Vân Ước just said, "Thank you."

26

She stopped for a moment, as she always did on her way home, on the bridge over the Yarra to peer into the water, thinking about Michael's advice. He was right. Of course he was. But so was she, to believe that there was more to Billy than most people saw. And it wasn't just that he was nice to his sister.

She hadn't shared with Michael the overheard conversation, or that she'd seen Billy reading one of her favorite books, *Dinner at the Homesick Restaurant* by Anne Tyler, with enjoyment up at Mount Fairweather. Because they would be weird admissions—that you had noted much about a boy from a discreet distance before he had even noticed that you existed.

Now, if she were confiding in Michael, she could add that the hyped bravado coexisted with vulnerability, that being funny was not the same as being happy, and that strength did not preclude tenderness.

At close range the river was coffee-colored, a silt-based river, though from a distance it reflected the myriad skies under which it stretched. The breeze was creating its own rippling topography of the water's surface.

There were a few rowing crews in the immediate vicinity, but not Billy's. She watched and admired the lean, well-oiled coordination, the crisp, strong movement of oars slicing the water. Another rich kids' sport, of course. Crowthorne Grammar's girls' and boys' first crews were invited to Henley, in England, later in the year. Imagine the fat family budget that allowed for something like that with nothing more than the ever-present *Congratulations! Well done!* These kids were always being stroked and caressed with soft words and extravagant praise, so different from her own mother's *don't waste time, study hard, practice more*—spoken at times perfunctorily, at other times sharply, like a slap or a bite.

• • •

Music to her ears, the whirring of a sewing machine greeted her as she unlocked her front door and walked in. Relief was short-lived as the machine stopped and her mother came out firing as soon as she heard the door.

"What is this about a tall boy? Who is this tall boy?"

"Who told you?"

"Everyone saw you. At first I said, Are you crazy? Not my

daughter! She is a serious girl. She is a good girl. There is a mistake."

"He's just a boy from my school."

"So, you—behind your parents' back—you arrange for a boy from your school to come here and to walk with you! Everyone saw!"

"I didn't know he was going to come here."

"He followed you?"

"No. No! Calm down. Can we sit down, please?" She was still standing just inside the front door with her bag on her back. "I'll make you a cup of tea and explain it all."

Her mother sat down reluctantly.

"Glad to see you're feeling a bit better today," Vân Ước said, sliding her bag onto the sofa and returning to face the music.

"Was. I *was*. Not now."

As she went from sink to kettle to cupboard and made tea, Vân Ước told her mother about Billy. At least, it was the version of Billy that had the best shot at making him an acceptable person to have in her life.

"Billy is a family friend of Eleanor's."

Her mother adored the homework club coordinator; they all did.

"How does he know Eleanor? He doesn't come to homework club."

"He just started. His father is a very important doctor. He is a friend of Eleanor's. And his mother, too, is a friend of Eleanor's."

"Why did he come here?"

"He didn't. He was in the street, running—he works very hard at his training; he is a leader of rowing—and he saw me coming from the apartments. We are in class together, and so it was polite, good manners, that he walked with me to school. Because he had finished his run."

"Running?"

"Yes." It was the weakest link in her story, but he had been wearing track clothes and was on his way to training, so in a pinch she might get away with it. The Eleanor story was safe. Her mother would never question Eleanor.

"Eleanor is very happy that Billy has started as a homework club tutor. She thinks he is a very responsible person. She asked him to help with the little ones."

"Why is he only starting just now?"

"He only just found out about it."

"Ah."

She put a steaming cup of jasmine tea in front of her mother and took a big breath.

"In fact, Billy is having some class members to his house this Saturday and I'm invited. Is that okay? Can I go? I'd be home early. No later than ten o'clock."

"No going out."

"Well, it's more like a school activity, really."

"Where is the notice from school?"

"No notice—it's just a celebration of the school's rowing."

"Why?"

"Because they're proud of their rowing achievements. So,

the rowers will be there, and some medals might be given out. Some speeches."

"Compulsory?"

"Not exactly, but the school expects us to go to at least one or two of these…informal events." Vân Ước tried to look as though it would be an unwanted burden to attend then played her trump card: "It's part of community life."

Community life was a very helpful expression, and she used it sparingly. She thought of it as her get-out-of-jail-free card. It was a strangely incomprehensible term to her parents, who thought of school purely as a seat of learning—a place of hard work and discipline and guaranteed excellent results that sent each student with a rocket down the glorious, well-paved, one-way street to university admission and an affluent professional life. Happily ever after. In Kew. *Community life* was an amorphous, misty zone. But they knew, because she had taken pains to point it out, that their daughter's scholarship depended in part on her being active in the school community and making a contribution to this *community life*.

She could see the gears and levers turning in her mother's brain. That was a partial win. The absence of an angry *no* meant the possibility of a provisional *yes*.

"You could always ask Eleanor about it," Vân Ước offered. "She understands how they like us to attend these things."

"I will talk with your *ba*," her mother said. "School uniform is worn?"

"I think we're allowed to wear casual clothes," Vân Ước said. "Like on casual clothes day."

"Ceremony, medals, speeches—prayers?"

"I'm sure there will be some prayers." That had to be true: some people would be praying to hook up with other people; at some stage of the night someone else would certainly be praying that they didn't vomit in a friend's parents' car on the way home...

"And to be held at the friends of Eleanor's, at their house? The doctor's house?"

"Yes. Billy's parents are the year level's official parent committee representatives." That bit was true at least. She knew from the school calendar notice that the parents' cocktail party held at the beginning of the year—an event her parents never attended—was scheduled to be held at Billy's place in two weeks.

"Hmmm. Sounds like a big waste of your time."

"Yes, I agree. But I should probably go."

Listen to that!/Bullshitting like a pro/This could be the start of a whole new level of parental manipulation.

The commentator dudes were right. That was uncomfortable—and it was the closest she had come, apart from taking art as a subject, to outright lying to her parents. She usually got by on selective truth-telling. The (conveniently modified) truth, the whole (conveniently modified) truth, and nothing but the (conveniently modified) truth. Fingers crossed and hope to die.

She went into her room and sat at her desk, first digging the winged cardigan from its hiding place in the wardrobe. It was as soothing to have on her knee as a favorite teddy bear might be. She patted one winged sleeve and imagined that the cardigan settled a bit more comfortably. "I'm going to have to put you back out there in a week or so," she said. "Wow. I'm speaking to a cardigan. Things are bad."

Lying to her mother/Talking to the cardigan/Watch, next thing she'll keep it and then Holly will be right/Thinks she can go along to the party without it backfiring/Has she learned nothing from us all these years?

27

Homework club on Friday came with the addition of Lou, with her freshly issued Working with Children permit, and Billy, who arrived ten minutes early and helped Vân Ước do a sweep of the playground area. Four needles. Three glue bags. Six siphons and some dead balloons. Heaps of cigarette butts.

Vân Ước partnered Lou with Saafi, a quiet year-six girl who needed lots of help with English, and particularly help with being brave enough to speak in a voice louder than a small whisper. She sent Saafi ahead to find a place at the table, and brought Lou up-to-date on how she was doing following the library bathroom meltdown.

"It turns out Billy isn't up to anything strange."

"So, what's up with all the stalky business?"

"I think it's possible he maybe does...like me."

Lou looked at her with frank disbelief. "Are you sure?"

"I know, but—yeah."

"So, the obvious question is...?" Lou was dubious.

Vân Ước nodded, worrying that she was playing the weirdest game of make-believe yet invented. "Yes. I do. I like him, too."

Lou looked over at Billy, who was gathering up a few more playground takers.

"Michael's not going to believe this. He can't stand those jock guys."

"He told me he doesn't think it's a good idea. I get it. It's not like jocks are my go-to people, either," Vân Ước said. As if she even had any go-to people, as such. "But it's possible he's different."

"Hmmm. Well, I guess we'll see. I couldn't have gone to his party anyway; Miro's got a gig."

"Sibylla said she'd go, but, really, I think it'll be okay." If terrifying social encounters for which you are in no way prepared were encompassed by the definition of *okay*.

"I'll let Sib know that you don't need her there. She didn't exactly want to bump into Holly." Lou was about to sit down when Jess came tearing in, late.

Vân Ước introduced the two girls, who smiled and greeted each other, before Lou went over to Saafi.

In a quick aside to Vân Ước, Jess said, "Your mum tells me you're going to a church-rowing-gathering at the house of the tall friend-of-Eleanor's-doctor-son who you accidentally ran into at our gate yesterday morning at seven a.m. because he was out running?"

"I didn't have much time to develop the story. There's a party at Billy's."

Jess gave Vân Ước her least impressed face, the one that looked like she'd tasted something disgusting and was about to spit. "I hope you know what you're putting your hand up for, lady."

Vân Ước was almost certain she was putting her hand up for something complicated and confusing that would probably end in tears (hers), but too late: it was already up.

"There were further developments yesterday," she said.

"Did these developments include any physical contact?"

"Yes. I'll fill you in tonight."

Toward the end of the hour, she saw Jess's student packing up and leaving a few minutes early, at which time Jess took her juice box and zipped straight outside to the playground.

• • •

If she thought her mother was dubious and unimpressed by the idea of Billy and his "celebration," it was nothing compared to the cool wrath of Jess after getting the full catch-up at their regular Friday movie night.

Kissing, she thought, was dodgy—because Billy hadn't passed her good-guy tests—but permissible; getting involved in a prank was another matter.

"It's so not *you*."

"I just set up the camera."

"And he's going to get the photo printed, rig it up in front of the CCTV camera, trick the staff and the security company, and you'll be expelled."

"Funny, though. Admit."

"Funny for him. His parents are paying thirty grand a year so he can misbehave. Not so funny for you, scholarship girl."

"He said he'd take the rap."

Jess shrugged. "It'll be nice to have you back at school with me. I can't wait."

"Too late to back out, anyway; I've already sent him the photos. He's getting a print made over the weekend."

They pondered the possible expulsion outcome, which Vân Ước wished she'd thought through better, and turned their attention to the large bowl of thick-cut homemade chips, made in Jess's mum's new fryer, the low-fat Frymatic that she'd bought at Aldi.

Jess got salt from the cupboard. *"Very disappointed! Bad, bad girl! You shame your family!"* she added in the parent-accent impersonation that they sometimes guilty-used in private.

At least the Billy friction was taking place in a world of crunchy salt-and-vinegar heaven.

They had *The Perks of Being a Wallflower.* And as well as their chip main course, they had chocolate bullets and Mars bar bites for dessert.

"Anyway, what were *you* talking to him about in such depth at the end of homework club?"

"I told him that he'd better remember me, because I'm your best friend. And he'd better read *Jane Eyre*, because that is the code by which you live your whole sorry life."

"What did he say?"

"He said okay."

"Anything else?"

"I said, *I hope you're not the douche who said 'oars before whores,'* because that would render him unworthy to tie your bootlaces."

"I told you he said it." Vân Ước resisted snapping, but Jess could be very intrusive without even trying. "What did he say then?"

"He admitted he'd said it—"

"Which you already knew."

Jess held up a hand. "But on reflection he could see it was very offensive. In fact, he'd unthinkingly picked it up from his father. Apparently, they said it back in his day. And he said you're doing a whole lot of gender politics stuff in Theory of Knowledge, and he's seeing the world in a new light."

"Wow. You got through a lot of material there."

"Got your back, babe."

"Anything else?"

"He said, *Good-bye, Jessica*—using my name very deliberately. And looking at me, so he'll remember next time."

"Sounds like he's making an effort, then."

"Effort will be measured next week. For now he is still officially blacklisted. And—I'm not kidding—I don't approve of you going to his party, with his idiot friends."

"I'm not even sure *I* approve. But I even more don't approve of you cross-examining him."

"Too late for that," said Jess. "You should never have chosen a bossy best friend when you were five."

"What are you, my mother?"

"You really are pissed. Are you?"

"A bit. Yes."

"Yeah, well, if you weren't dating a dick, I never would've *had* to cross-examine him."

Vân Ước's annoyance was mirrored in Jess's expression. This was the closest she and Jess had ever come to fighting, and it felt horrible.

28

Vân Ước woke up with a burst of adrenaline the morning of party day, tried not to think about last night's disagreeable exchange with Jess, and was out the door by 6 a.m. for a run.

She came home and showered.

She changed her sheets and did some laundry.

She got through forty-five minutes of oboe practice, doing heaps of work on long notes and scales, and did as much homework as she could manage before lunch.

She texted Billy and wished him luck for the race—which, it turned out, was a series of races, first heats and then a final.

She supervised her mother's tablet-taking.

She got her parents together for a three-way eye-contact

meeting in the kitchen at lunchtime to dissuade them from coming along to the art briefing at school next week.

She worked her shift at Henry Ha Minh Rolls.

She and Jess treated themselves to a two-straw three-flavor Slurpee from the 7-Eleven on the way home, which (sort of) broke the ice of their cross (for them) words from the night before.

She spent an hour experimenting with filters on one disk image, and saved the file of comparative images to print later as a process note for her journal. Always, now, keeping in the back of her mind, *What does it mean to me?*

She showered again, sent out a prayer of thanks to the pimple gods that she was breakout-free, washed her hair, brushed it out, and sat down for a couple more hours of homework. Before she could settle to that, she spent (wasted) at least fifteen minutes rifling through her tragically understocked wardrobe, wondering what on earth she could wear to the party. She thought it should probably be a skimpy dress with spaghetti straps and high heels, like the outfits she'd seen in party photos her Reynolds housemates had pinned up last year, but she didn't have anything like that in her wardrobe. Even if she had, her parents wouldn't let her out wearing clothes like that.

And she was back to square one. How to fit in? What to wear—if not to look good, then at least to look inconspicuous? Billy had said it was a barbecue. That sounded quite casual. Maybe she could get away with wearing jeans. She didn't feel close enough to anyone at school to call and ask, despite Lou and Sibylla's kindness. It was a girlfriend conversation. Not a person-sticking-up-for-persecuted-underdog-classmate conversation. And she couldn't call Jess, because Jess's resolved position until Billy had proved himself worthy was firm disapproval. The best outfit solution was, sadly, still just the jeans and orange top she'd worn for casual clothes day the week before.

Billy had texted back, *Rulers of the universe. See you later.*

He'd said people were coming any time from seven on, so she figured if she left home at quarter to, she'd get there around quarter past and that would be okay.

As she was dressing, she heard her dad's boss, Bác Bảo, arrive. Odd timing. Bác Bảo was part of the Friday dinner group, and he and her father played cards every second Wednesday. Like clockwork. Saturday night did not figure in their relationship.

"Bảo and I will take you to your community service night," her dad said as she emerged from her room.

"It's fine—I can get the tram," she said.

"No problem. All organized," Bác Bảo said. "The van's downstairs."

"Let's go," said her dad. "You've got the address?"

Vân Ước looked at the three smiling faces and knew there was no getting out of this one.

Her mother gave her a kiss-push-out-the-door.

She was going to be arriving at Billy's party underdressed, too early, in a van that said *Bảo's Happy Chickens* with graphics of, yes, very happy-looking cartoon chickens painted on its sides, and a large 3-D model happy chicken on the roof of the van.

Before this moment of new hell, the van had only ever been a vague philosophical conundrum: How could the chickens be happy, given that they were dead and destined for the dinner table? Now, it had been transformed into a weapon of torture designed for her personal mortification. She was spending a night in reverse-Cinderella land.

She sat in the front, perched up high in the traffic, nice and visible, beside her dad and Bác Bảo. She leaned her back in hard to the seat, as though it might decide to be kind and swallow her whole. Fortunately, the van was refrigerated, so there was only a minimal pong of chicken, tinged by the bleach used to scrub it out.

She directed Bác Bảo to pull in at the corner of Billy's street with only the smallest glimmer of hope, because, as she feared, they insisted on delivering her to the house, so they would know where to pick her up.

She had a wave of nauseated anxiety when she imagined her father might want to come in and check out the community life rowing ceremony. Her cover would be blown and her parents would never let her out of the door again.

"Bye," she said firmly, jumping down.

"We will be back at ten. Be ready."

"Thanks," she said, only daring to look around as they pulled away, with a blast of diesel this street would never before have experienced, once she was safely inside the (thankfully, unlocked) gate. It must be her lucky day. The coast was clear of mean girls.

One bullet dodged. But straight into the path of another.

29

Arriving at the front door, also open, she tried and failed to locate a bell or buzzer, and was about to lift the hand-shaped knocker when an elegant woman walked across the hallway and paused as she saw Vân Ước. She looked puzzled, clearly wondering who this girl was, standing in her doorway. She was not a Tiff, or a Pippa—a girl whose parents one knew. Vân Ước didn't have mind-reading skills, but it was fairly obvious what Billy's mother was thinking in the moment before an appropriately warm smile of greeting appeared on her subtly frozen face.

Billy came leaping down the stairs, barefoot, in jeans, hair hanging down in its characteristic wet tangle. She'd have to give him the low-down on the towel-dry one day. She was pretty sure he must just shake his head, like a dog, when he got out of the shower. She frowned—*must not think about Billy in the shower.* Too distracting for a walk through the minefield of his parent-inhabited house.

"Vân Ước! Great—you're so early. You've met my mum? Abi."

Vân Ước smiled, made eye contact, and held out her hand to shake hands with Abi, as Debi had taught her to do. "How do you do?" she said. People like Abi expected some formality, a straight-line version of Anglo good manners, which, to them, were simply "good manners." In Vân Ước's family, arms folded across the stomach and a gentle bow was the well-mannered greeting to an older person.

"Lovely to meet you, Vân Ước. Do join us in the garden. You're our very first guest."

Billy gave Vân Ước a friendly eye roll, as though to say, *Yeah, I know, full on,* and they followed his mother outside.

Mel appeared with a massive platter of gourmet-looking sausages. She smiled and said hello to Vân Ước, and started tonging sausages onto an equally massive barbecue hot plate.

"I don't know about your mother, Vân Ước," Abi said, "but *I've* found that if there's a large group of young men about to arrive, who might also be having a beer, it's a very good idea to have loads of sausages and bread ready to go."

Vân Ước just smiled. Her mother had nearly flipped her lid when one young man was reported to be in the general vicinity of their apartment; a large number of them turning up might cause spontaneous combustion.

"I don't think I've met your parents yet, have I? Are you

new to Melbourne? A corporate transfer? From Singapore, perhaps?"

"Mum, don't be such a stickybeak. Vân Ước's family lives in Melbourne. She was born here. You don't know *everyone* in Melbourne."

"You'd be surprised, darling."

"I'll tell you three things about Vân Ước. She duxed honors math last year, equal with Michael Cassidy (whose parents you do know), she duxed French, and she is the best art student in our year."

Vân Ước could see Billy's mother assessing her in a blink; she was a scholarship social nonentity, and Abi was far from impressed to hear the three things. Whereas *she* was astounded that Billy had registered anything at all about her that predated the fateful creative writing class.

The doorbell rang. "And that's all you're getting," said Billy, bending down and giving his mother a quick kiss. "And don't forget you said you and Dad were going to be out tonight."

"And we are, but we'll be back before midnight, by which time we expect you to be saying good-bye to your guests and settling down for some sleep after such a big day."

"Sure."

Billy took Vân Ước's hand, a gesture that delivered some much-needed reassurance, and which she saw Abi register immediately, as new arrivals flowed into the garden, greeting Abi and Mel, helping themselves to drinks, and setting up a volume of chatter that would continue to grow.

"Vince, can you chuck on some music, buddy?" Billy asked.

Vân Ước could see that Vincent was thrilled to be the one selected; he headed back inside, fiddling with his iPod, and very soon Chet Faker was filtering through the French doors.

She sat in a garden chair in the shadows for ages. She felt like a shadow. Billy was so much the center of things; his crew members were elated at the day's triumph—this regatta vindicated the grueling training regimen they'd been subjected to all summer. The guys, she saw, had mostly come preloaded, as they called it in media reports on underage drinking, so they were more than half pissed and could afford to drink at what looked like a moderate rate at their friend's house. Naturally, she couldn't drink; her parents would have a complete meltdown if she came home with alcohol on her breath.

Lots of them would go out clubbing after the party, armed with fake IDs, and keep up the drinking. She wondered how their bodies could stand it. She knew from ambient school chat that Billy's were the sort of parents who would let other parents know that they'd be serving some alcohol, and it would be up to individual families as to whether that was okay. But once a critical mass had arrived, it was a free-for-all, and surely the parents knew that and blind-eyed it. When she looked at the ice-filled metal tubs decoratively placed on tables and laden with beers and bottled mixed vodkas, the girls' preferred drink, she was amazed that anyone ever made it to school on Mondays.

Billy finally managed to penetrate the wall of people and reached her just as his father appeared at the doorway into the house.

His presence was electric. Like Billy's mother, this guy was a perfectly polished magazine version of "parent." He oozed authority. Billy broke away from her, with obvious regret, and went over to stand next to his father, who looked at him with pride and ownership, but no apparent warmth. Vân Ước got the feeling, looking at them together, that it could be this relationship that fueled Billy's restlessness.

They looked like superior beings framed in the backlit glow of the French doors.

It clicked for her, the thing about Billy—he was no longer comfortable in the role he'd been assigned. He looked the part. He knew it perfectly. It just didn't play so well anymore.

"Guys, a quick word," Billy's father said to the crowd. The noise died down. "Congratulations for today. You rowed like the winners you are. We're going to kill it this year! Here, and then in England. Row, Crowthorne!"

Vân Ước nearly jumped out of her skin to hear the whole group yell back, *Row, Crowthorne!* This must be what they all did standing on riverbanks at regattas. A whole new world. A strange world.

"I DIDN'T HEAR YOU," shouted Billy's father.

"ROW, CROWTHORNE! ROW, ROW, ROW! ROW, CROWTHORNE!"

"That's more like it. Party here after Head of the River—it'll be a third-generation win in this house, so the least we can do is buy the drinks."

He raised a hand in farewell and disappeared to hoots and whoops of approval. Someone turned the music up.

She heard the inevitable bitchy comment about her clothes: "Check out Vân Ước. She's come as a dude."

Dude, fraud, misfit—sure, that was about right; the shape of not fitting in was almost comfortably familiar.

She held a glass of mineral water and moved about the terrace as though she were looking for someone. A strong pang of wishing for Jess swept through her, and she wondered where little glass vials were when you needed them.

The world was full of contradictions and things that couldn't be explained. The interesting edge of science was located at that point: trying to explain the inexplicable. Making the intuitive leap. It was where all the creativity happened in that field.

She castigated herself; a dumb wish wasn't science—it wasn't anything close. Puzzling over it for the umpteenth time, she still couldn't come up with a theory to explain why this was happening, but what she was feeling was real, happening in the physical world, not just in her imagination.

Even at the opposite end of the terrace from Billy, she was conscious of his awareness of her. The party was keeping them apart, but he was moving toward her as though she had gravitational pull. It wasn't natural. Unless you were a planet.

It was obvious, unavoidable: Vân Ước had to find the writer who taught that class and ask her about the vial. But how could she even broach such a ridiculous topic? *You know that little vial in the creative prompts box? Have you ever heard of* unexplained magical events *following its use by a student?* Please! Who was she kidding? It wouldn't be possible to say such stupid words out loud. And how would she even find her?

She paused beside a table, under a tree, checked her watch and looked around, as though she expected someone she knew to arrive at any second.

"Hey."

Finally! Someone was going to talk to her. It was Vincent. She was pleased and, even though she didn't like him, she smiled. He was going to make her look normal. A normal, partygoing, socialized person.

"Can you move? I can't reach..." He stretched an arm past her as she stepped sideways. She was blocking his access to the beer.

"Sorry." She looked for Billy. He was still being waylaid. She smiled in response to his apologetic grimace. It was like one of those horrible dreams when you want something to happen but it's all slowed down and ends up being unattainable. Time for a bathroom visit. Surely that could kill ten or fifteen minutes.

● ● ●

By the time she emerged from the bathroom in response to someone banging on the door, the music had been turned up again, and the French doors framed a group of girls dancing with arms up in the air, shouting along with Taylor Swift. She stayed inside and stood on the edge of a group. She smiled, listened, and tried to look interested, but no one acknowledged that she was there, or said anything to include her in the conversation, so she slipped away and found herself in the entrance hallway of the house.

She headed outside to the front garden. Why not just walk home and tell her parents someone gave her a lift? What a relief to have that brain wave. There was no rule that said she had to stay. Billy could have tried harder to reach her sooner. Longing looks only got you so far.

Groan, Holly and Pippa were standing like sentinels on either side of the gate.

"Hi, Vân Ước," said Pippa. "How *are* you?" She was drunk.

"Hi."

"Tell me"—she leaned in, then turned sideways to blow her smoke away from Vân Ước—"do you get back to China much? Because I *love* Shanghai. Love. It."

"My family actually came from Vietnam, originally."

"Oh, gosh, sorry. Well, Hội An is beautiful, too."

"So I hear. I haven't been."

"Are you going away this year, Pippa?" asked Holly, grinding out her cigarette on the flagstone path.

"Sicily in September. My parents are so boring. What about you?"

"We're not even leaving the country. Port Douglas. My parents are so tight." Holly looked at Vân Ước. "What's up—lover boy ignoring you? Has he hooked up with someone else? What did you expect? Is the guy who lives here really going to go out with someone who works in a paper hygiene hat?"

That was it. He'd asked her to his stupid party. She'd been snubbed, ignored, bored, and now insulted. She was going back in there, and if he wasn't available immediately, she was going home. Surely by now he'd been stopped and hugged and congratulated and had chatted and joked with every stupid person there.

They almost collided, he entering the house from the terrace, and she returning there.

He put his arms around her, moving to the music. "All I wanted tonight was some time with you, and here it is, finally."

She looked up into his eyes. "Why do you think I'd want to dance with someone who thinks it's cool when little birds get electrocuted?"

He laughed in protest. "Way to trash a romantic moment. It wasn't that the little bird got fried; it was the odds. I mean, what are the odds? Come on, it's never going to happen, is it? But it did."

"Probably something like the odds of us going out."

"Nuh, that was a sure thing."

"Take a look around and see what your friends think about it."

Billy looked around and, of course, saw nothing but smiles. She was the one getting greased off in private.

"They'll get used to it," he said, leaning down and kissing her.

She pulled away. Public kissing. This was so far outside her experience, she couldn't even begin to tell him the number of ways it made her uncomfortable. She failed hard all the way around the social merry-go-round.

"I've got to go" was what she managed to say.

"Right now? Really?"

"Yup, well, soon. I'm being picked up."

He looked annoyed. A whole party had eaten him up like ice cream, but the one thing he wanted wasn't available.

"Hey, I was lucky to be able to come at all."

"I'll walk you out, then, I guess."

They headed out through the house and she let go of Billy's hand in the front garden. By the time they were halfway down the path, they were a respectable distance apart. She could see the chicken-mobile through the gate. She should have realized; of course her father and Bác Bảo would arrive early.

Holly came hurrying in from the street, where she'd been smoking again, if smell was anything to go by. "Billy, there's some super-suspicious-looking Asians in a van parked right outside your place. They've been lurking there for ten minutes."

Vân Ước recognized this as another perfect test of Billy's infatuation. It killed her to keep engaging with an idea she rejected, but surely only magic would get Billy past the social faux pas of going out with a girl who rode in the Happy Chickens chariot.

"Don't worry; it's my father. He works for the man driving the van. They're here to pick me up."

"Can you say sorry to your dad if we've kept him waiting?" said Billy.

Vân Ước and Holly looked at Billy with competing levels of disbelief.

"Sure," said Vân Ước, smiling. "See you on Monday."

"Should I come out and say hi?" Billy asked.

"Maybe next time," Vân Ước said, enjoying Holly's gaping surprise.

Vân Ước walked out the gate, opened the passenger-side door of the van, and climbed in. Her father would never register that the tone in which the smoking girls on the footpath said, "Good night, Vân Ước," and, "See you, Vân Ước," was coated with insincere smarm.

She was going home in an unapologetic pumpkin. Her clothes had been clearly inappropriate all night. But she didn't need to rush out or even to leave a sneaker behind. Unless the whateverthehellitwas expired over the weekend, Billy would know exactly where to find her on Monday morning.

She was expecting to have to explain to her father, and Bác Bảo, why her classmates were smoking on the footpath at the rowing ceremony dressed in skimpy evening dresses, so it was like getting a free kick when, instead, they expressed their disappointment that the teachers would smoke at an official school function. Thank heavens for too much hair and makeup. Those girls did look more like twenty-five than seventeen. And her father was clueless about what girls like these typically wore on any occasion.

30

Safely in her room after deflecting and half answering her parents' questions about the school event, she patted the winged cardigan good night (was that getting strange?), got into bed, and did the gentle four-knock to Jess: *Are you awake?* No answer. Jess was ignoring her. No way was she was asleep at ten thirty—for sure she was awake and reading.

It felt so different having Billy as her private number one fantasy mew, never expecting it to cross over into real life, and having Billy actually like her. The whole aura around him liking her was so insulting. How many times could she stand to encounter the face of someone who couldn't believe Billy liked Vân Ước? Tears burned in her eyes. How dare they be so surprised? She was as nice as anyone else. And smarter. But had she really let anyone see her? Was it partly her fault for preferring to slip through as unnoticed as possible? Maybe to his friends it was as though he was going out with the invisible woman.

But she knew it was more than that, worse than that. It was their rejection of Billy slumming it with someone so far removed from his born-to-rule class. There. She'd used the word. It was a class thing. Which also meant a money thing. And they were both related to the refugee thing. Their judging and ranking made her hackles rise. Part of her relished the idea of standing up in front of all the people she least liked at school, and shouting, *He wanted* me, *but I rejected* him. *Because I'm not buying into that bullshit.*

She rolled over, untwisting her nightie as she turned, flipping her pillow over to its cool side. She gave it a good punch and thought through it all again—it was running on a loop—the whole preposterous, fallacious, spurious basis on which Billy liked her. That was some bullshit she was readily buying into, she coolly observed of herself, from the disapproving outside.

Well, it's not as though he'd like her in her own right, would he?/ Ha ha ha ha ha ha. Good one/Of course it's the wish hoo-ha.

How could her pride allow that to stand? It couldn't, clearly. Or not for long. But why shouldn't she have a couple of weeks knowing what it felt like to go out with Billy? Was she even more superficial than that? Did she just want to go out with "a" Billy?

She buried her face in the pillow. She knew it was a cheat. No way would Jane approve.

191

It was like the day in primary school, year three, when her father, in an unprecedented move, had brought home a big bag of gummy bears and she'd been allowed to take them to school. She had instant sticky friends for playtime and lunchtime. She knew they loved her for her gummy bears, but she still enjoyed it while it lasted.

31

On Monday morning the lockers seemed to have been waiting for her to arrive. There was a picture of a chicken stuck on the front of her locker, which she decided to ignore and take down when the area was less crowded.

Holly made a clucking noise when Vân Ước opened her locker to put her bag in. Billy arrived to hear the clucking. He walked over to Holly.

"What did you say?"

"Nothing."

"What's this?" Billy ripped the chicken picture from Vân Ước's locker. "Who the fuck put this here?"

People turned away and got busy with doors and books and bags and locks.

"I'm going to guess it was the person clucking, then." Billy handed the screwed-up ball of paper to Holly.

"Billy, are you for real?" she asked. "Since when did you get so weird and lose your sense of humor? You would have been making the same joke back when you were normal."

Vân Ước took a deep breath. "If you want to joke about it, go ahead. My father works in a chicken-processing plant. He doesn't drive, or own a car. His boss offered to drop me at Billy's and pick me up on Saturday night. I was lucky to be allowed out at all. My parents don't particularly believe in students having a social life."

Holly didn't say anything else, but her face was set in a sneer.

Billy held Vân Ước's hand, but he was looking at the assembled group. Ben walked in as Billy said: "What a pack of losers. Do you really think that because your parents have money, or their parents did, that you're better than Vân Ước or her parents? You didn't make the money. It's random. It's dumb luck. Let's see what you do yourself. Let's take a look in ten years."

He directed the next comment squarely at Holly. "And it's pretty easy to see that some people are so pathetic that all they will have done is buy clothes and prance around like idiots. Talking about clothes. With other idiots." Vintage mean-Billy.

Ben had been looking on with apparent incredulity as things blew up. "Lighten up, dude," he said.

"Fuck off, dude," Billy said.

"What about you, Billy? Won't you just be another dull doctor who briefly went out with a povvo Asian girl at school to piss off his parents?" Holly's voice was shaking. She obviously felt she had to retaliate, but she clearly didn't feel comfortable turning against someone like Billy, even in self-defense.

Billy looked at Holly with freezing disdain. "Wrong on both scores. Surprise, surprise."

Holly gave Vân Ước a look of pure hostility as she walked past, as though to say, *Look at the trouble you've caused.*

If Holly knew how transitory her going out with Billy was likely to be, she wouldn't waste the frown repetitions getting angry about it. Vân Ước wished she could go home. Couldn't she have the occasional "mental health day" her classmates took from time to time? It seemed to be a day at home being pampered and not having to turn up at school, despite being perfectly well. Her parents wouldn't even understand the concept. Her sick days were hard enough to come by when she was half dead.

Holly's nasty comment was still stinging; Vân Ước had never considered that Billy's motivation for going out with her might simply be to annoy his parents.

• • •

By lunchtime, things seemed to have settled sufficiently that there was another bout of the ongoing Jenga tournament. Billy was still undefeated. Vân Ước was uncomfortably aware of Holly, Tiff, Ava, and Gabi vipering quietly in a huddle. No doubt talking about her—in their eyes, a thief, of cardigans and boys. An unworthy interloper. She half watched Jenga, feeling glum, while she ate her lunch, then went to the library.

She and Jess always ridiculed the role of girlfriend-to-the-jock on movie nights. Too sidekick to be interesting, and it turned out to be true. The concept of looking on from the sidelines and cheering was not something she'd ever feel okay about. Plus, it was half an hour better spent reading.

● ● ●

Sibylla and Lou and Michael were already in the library. Michael and Lou were playing chess; Sibylla was flicking though a pile of magazines.

"Escaping Jenga?" she asked.

"It's a bit loud to read in there," said Vân Ước.

Lou looked up. "I can't wait till it ends, the Jenga thing. It's the bro-dudes building the world, and destroying the world. Too much like real life to be funny."

Vân Ước smiled in agreement and headed to the quiet study area.

● ● ●

It felt impossible that Vân Ước could be more in love with Sylvia Plath, but after finding "Mad Girl's Love Song" she was. Written when Plath was twenty. Genius. She looked up to see Billy walking toward her and sighed.

"You disappeared—I thought you were still in the common room. I remain, yours truly, king of the Jenga world."

"I'm so happy for you."

"Oooh, the Vân Ước low-key stinging sarcasm."

"Well. Jenga."

"Hey, I'm so sorry about all the chicken stuff this morning."

"It wasn't your fault. It's not your sorry."

"I don't want anyone being mean to you."

"And I don't want to cause trouble with your friends."

"You're not the one causing trouble." Looking at her books, he said, "Don't forget, Sylvia part two, at mine on Wednesday."

"Even with your parents there?"

"They won't be home by then. Wouldn't matter if they were."

"I don't know how thrilled your mother would be..."

"If she knew we were going out?"

Wow. He'd said it out loud.

"We are?"

"To the extent that we can, given that you're not allowed out much, and you don't want me to come to your place. And you obviously object to public displays of affection."

"Wouldn't you like to check in with me? Ask me if I want to go out with you?"

He looked shocked. "Don't you?"

It cracked her up that the idea of a girl maybe not wanting to go out with him was utterly alien to his experience. "Sure. I guess. If you can cope with all the limitations."

"That is the most excellent news I could hear. Ever."

"But don't get too excited, because from the look on your mother's face when we met..."

Billy dismissed her misgivings with a shrug. "My parents don't like anything that distracts me from study or rowing."

"Ha. My parents don't like anything that distracts me from study or study."

"We've got heaps in common, you and me."

"I."

"I'm going to get the common room print done tonight. Maybe we could put it up early on Thursday."

"Okay."

● ● ●

Vân Ước was missing Jess. She stopped by after school. Jess opened the door with mashed avocado spread all over her face. She liked the occasional all-natural face mask. At least this one wouldn't set like a rock, unlike the fateful, supposedly oil-absorbing oatmeal mask.

"Why are you mad about Billy before it's absolutely warranted?"

"Hello to you, too."

"He might be okay."

"Unlikely, but. How was the party?"

"Pretty good. His parents and his friends hate me. And we only got to kiss for about one minute before my dad came to pick me up. *In Bác Bảo's van.*"

Jess clapped a hand over her mouth in disbelief. "Classy move. What did he make of that?" She rinsed avocado from her hand at the kitchen sink.

"Didn't miss a beat."

Jess raised her avocado-y eyebrows. "Well, that's one point for him."

"He's been winning plenty of points. The question is, why?"

"You're not still thinking it's got anything to do with that stupid teacher's stupid glass vial stupid wish thing, are you?"

"I think I've got to try and find the teacher."

"And out yourself as completely wacko?"

"I was thinking more, ask a couple of open-ended questions."

"Like, 'Anything *strange* ever happened to *anyone* in *any* of your classes *evah*?'"

"You don't have to tell me how ridiculous it is."

"Don't do it!"

"I have to. Otherwise, it's the most massive cheat. And how can I honestly let myself like someone who has been wishmagic-ed into liking me?"

"I'd have Jennifer Lawrence on wishmagic terms any day."

"You wouldn't. You'd want her to like you for real."

"I'm not that fussy."

"You know she likes boys, right?"

"Of course I know. It doesn't really matter, seeing as how I'm not ever likely to meet her and all."

"You know the cardigan I found?"

"That's magic, too?" Jess could be very judgmental.

"No, but I like to pat it. And I talk to it occasionally. It seems to have a personality."

"You're telling me this why?"

"Who else would I tell?"

Jess got a skewer from the cutlery drawer and started gently poking it through her mask.

"Itchy?"

"Very."

"Wash it off."

"I've got five more minutes."

"You might as well scrape it off with crackers."

"Don't worry. I thought about it."

"But?"

"But if it's been drawing out impurities from my complexion, I'd be eating avocado with a nice dose of impurity. Which is pus, I presume, in a best-case scenario—that is, if it's worked."

"Mmmm, delicious. So what are we watching on Friday?"

"Sally Thomasetti's lending me *Say Anything*."

"Omigod, I'm dying to see that. That's the last item on our *I can't believe you haven't seen it* list, isn't it?"

"Yup. And we can review Billy's performance at homework club."

"And figure out how I find the creative writing teacher."

"Directory?"

"True."

"But please don't. Dignity."

"I know. But I—I don't know what else I can do."

"Just get back in touch with the rational girl who lives in there." Jess pointed to Vân Ước's forehead.

"Wise words, avocado-face."

"Hey, at least I don't talk to cardigans."

Vân Ước got up and stretched, picked up her bag, and headed for the door.

"You study hard, now," said Jess.

32

Because her oboe teacher had been called away at short notice to attend the birth of his third child, Vân Ước had spare time after school on Wednesday before going to Billy's. She took some David Foster Wallace essays to the part of the river where school and university boat sheds congregated, and found a bench in the shade of a plane tree.

Billy's crew was going to be doing sprint training, so she'd see him row for the first time, and maybe get a glimpse of what all the fuss was about.

She got out her camera, put on a telephoto lens, and looked idly through the viewfinder. After all the rain and the heat, the riverbanks were deep green and smelled sweetly of grass. A bicycle crunched along the track. It was Billy's coach, the head of rowing, Mr. Robertson, holding a compact megaphone and shouting unintelligible things like, "Speed up the catch. Hughes, YOU'RE LATE. Square up earlier."

She trained her camera on the crew. They didn't appear to be slacking off. These boys were working as hard as she'd ever seen human bodies work. They'd transformed themselves into a machine, made of muscle and rhythm and—what? What could possibly motivate them to push themselves like this? Ambition? Determination? Pride? Or was it enough that, to them, being dropped from the most prestigious crew in the school would be unthinkable?

Billy and Ben Capaldi were the only two year elevens in the first eight. The other crew members and the cox were year twelves. She recognized them, but didn't know any of them.

Ben was concentrating so intently she could feel it even from the bank. Sheer, brutal willpower was driving him. But Billy looked angry, as though harnessing every negative emotion to fuel the relentless repetition of the stroke.

She walked down the embankment to the edge of the water to be closer to the crew's level, and shot a series of stills as they rowed. She'd give them to the editor of the school newsletter— contributing-to-community-life bonus.

As well as all the evident mental exertion, she could certainly see great beauty in the harmony of what they were doing. Beauty, too, in the way Billy seemed so easily, so perfectly, suited to the sport. Born to row. His muscled arms; wide, square shoulders; and long legs seemed purpose-built—

and, she supposed, in a sense, that's exactly what training did: build this body to move that long boat through the water.

When the cox called, "Easy. Rest," and the boys relaxed and stretched backward, their faces broke out in grimaces of relief and grins of satisfaction that were short-lived. The coach was yelling back at them, "Let's have a set of sprints from here to Princes Bridge. On Jonno's count."

● ● ●

Walking back to Billy's, she felt autumn's incipience in the warm afternoon, a whisper that the early evening might be cooler than the string of hot nights they'd had for the last few weeks.

"You know when you shower after training...?"

"Yeah."

"What, if anything, do you do with your hair?"

He put a hand up, grabbed a handful of hair, and gave it a squeeze. "Nothing. I guess I sort of pull it together, like a ponytail, squeeze it, and then I shake my head. That's about it."

"I figured."

"Low maintenance."

She smiled at him. He sure was Mr. Careless Magnificence. No preening or vanity. Or maybe the vanity was so deeply assured it didn't need constant reinforcement. Interesting.

"What do you do with your hair?"

She laughed. "Pretty similar, actually. I insert a quick towel-dry before I brush it and let it air-dry. I can't be faffed spending time with a blow-dryer."

"We're so hair-compatible. We should go out. Oh, wait…"

"What are you thinking about when you row?"

"I'm not thinking; it's pure physical effort."

"No, but where is your head?"

"I'm not kidding; it's just—for me, anyway—100 percent concentrated, in the moment, in the body. Or I'd fuck it up."

"So, what's the good bit?"

"Winning."

"Why?"

"All the work's paid off."

"Huh."

"You know, it's like lots of sport; it's not an intellectual thing."

"And yet it's what'll get you to Brown."

"If I do well enough academically."

"Of course you'll do well. You're smart; you will excel. That's what Crowthorne Grammar does. It's an excel factory."

"But with a heart."

"That's part of the excel—the human, well-rounded angle."

"True. Anyway, I'll definitely excel now I've got you as my English partner."

"That's not for keeps; it's only for our first oral prep."

Billy leaned in, arm around her waist, and kissed her; as they walked on, he held her hand in his engulfing, calloused grip.

"How am I going—breaking down the PDA resistance?"

"I'm still resistant. But back to rowing—what is it that you love? It must be love, right? It takes up so much of your life."

She imagined that whatever it was that pulled him out of bed at such ungodly hours must be, to him, something as desirable as art was to her.

Billy looked thoughtful, and dubious. "I don't know that I *love* it. It's just always been there—my dad rowed in the first eight, and my grandfather, and so do I. I like it when we're flying along. The rhythm. If I can forget the pain. And you get used to that. You can put the pain in a different part of your head and ignore it."

"You're a machine."

"Yeah, baby."

"I'm not a baby."

"But you're a babe."

"Nuh-uh. Is *anything* we're talking about in Theory of Knowledge sinking in?"

"Of course it is," he said, rethinking. "You're—beautiful?"

"That's more acceptable, so long as you don't *just* love me for my beauty." She was being flippant, but felt embarrassed that the L word had slipped out in this particular context.

"I don't," he said. "Despite your beauty being…great…it's the least of the reasons I love you."

They walked along a few more steps.

Surely *now* she would hear a shimmer of fairy bells. Come on, cue magic SFX. He'd actually said those words? That had to be wish-induced. If his parents knew what he'd just said, they'd probably have her banished from the city. Or at least from the school.

"Wow," he said. "That was a bit intense. Sorry. I've never said *that* before." He broke out into a huge smile; he leaned down, and they kissed again, and worry about being affectionate in public was the last thing on her mind.

• • •

Mel was like something from old American TV make-believe land. This afternoon, in that pristine kitchen, sat a plateful of homemade chocolate chip biscuits, and another of chilled grapes and strawberries. Moving through the house was a little more fraught now that Vân Ước had met the parents, but they made it upstairs with no sightings.

• • •

Kissing Billy was like discovering a many-petaled, deep, complicated flower with her mouth. First, his lips, smooth and strong. She'd never thought of lips as strong or weak, but his expressed such confident intention. They moved over her face and mouth and neck as though with a true compass. These lips were surrounded by rasping whiskers. She touched her fingertips along his jawline and felt the direction of the whiskers change. So alien and beautiful. They created their own growth pattern. There was a tiny whorl under the end of the jawbone on the left side of his face.

"Do I need a shave?" Billy whispered.

"I don't know. I like the way your face feels."

"How does it feel?"

She considered this for a while. "Strange, but good."

Then there was his open mouth. She loved the taste of him—the inside of his mouth was an unexpectedly great place to be. The whole thing disconcertingly reminded her of the mew; she put it out of her head. Right now, if there were an animal noise she might make, it would be a demanding growl, which might be a bit frightening; perhaps better all-around if she avoided animal sounds. At least until they'd known each other a bit longer.

Surely kissing like this couldn't be very far removed on the Richter scale from what actual sex must be like. They were inside each other in a seductively involving way, being pulled through concentric circles of longing to the deep center of things.

They were lying on his bed now, watching and touching each other, aching, entranced. The maybe-probably-impossible-wish had become a nagging backbeat of anxiety, but this—this was real-world magic, a spell insistently weaving them together.

The idea of drowning in someone's eyes had always seemed too silly for words. Not anymore. Not now that she knew Billy's eyes. The outer circle of each blue iris was thick and black; the blueness, at close range, was assembled from myriad fractured facets; his lashes and eyebrows were dark and defined.

It felt as though she might have been kissing Billy Gardiner for a thousand days and that they would keep kissing forever. When he put his hand under her dress and up, gently, between her legs, she held it there, and moved against it until she came. He didn't take his eyes off her face, and she only squeezed her eyes shut because she couldn't not.

She'd barely had time to wonder how they'd so quickly

leapfrogged to *here*, or worry that she had no idea how to return the favor, and that he would soon know the full extent of her sexual cluelessness, when there were three sharp knocks on his bedroom door, making them both sit up quickly, trying to breathe normally.

Billy picked up a book and said, "Yeah?"

His mother came in. "Hello, darling. Hello…"

"Vân Ước," said Billy.

"Of course: Vân Ước."

"Hi."

How must this look to Billy's mother? They were both in full school uniform; neither of them had even one button undone. Her dress was on the slightly too-big side, loose and almost knee-length. Billy's books and folder were on the bed, and so were hers. It kind of looked like they'd been working there. They *had* been working there. Before they were kissing there. The only giveaway was her school shoes. Off, next to the bed. And perhaps their flushed faces.

Billy's mother seemed to be talking to Vân Ước's shoes, those guilty little islands on the floor. "I just popped up to say it's nearly dinnertime. Would Vân Ước like to stay, or does she need to be getting home?"

"Thank you—Abi—but I'd better get going." She looked at her watch. It was later than she'd realized.

"What a shame. Perhaps another time."

The way Abi said *what a shame* reminded her of Tiff and Holly's *sorry*. And she guessed *another time* might be when hell froze over.

33

Vân Ước just smiled when she saw Billy at the gate so early the next morning. Last week was outrage and suspicion. This week was irrationality and going with the wish flow. How far she'd traveled from the land of common sense.

Billy glanced up at the windows of the apartments and risked giving her the swiftest kiss on the cheek.

They walked along Albert Street, talking. Billy was ridiculously pleased about the common room prank he was about to set up, then he wanted to hear all about her portfolio work, and she admitted that she hadn't told her parents about her plans to study art.

"Nice con," he said.

"It's not exactly a con; I wouldn't need to be selective

truth-telling if I had normal parents." It felt disloyal to speak of her parents in those terms, but as far as her study choices went, her parents weren't normal.

"No such thing," Billy said absently. "Not that I've ever come across, anyway."

Closer to school, Billy stopped at a cafe to get a takeaway coffee. "What would you like?"

"I'm okay."

As they entered the small and, to her, intimidatingly cool place, Billy started ordering, "Can I please get a large double-shot…"

"…latte, to take away," said the man making coffee.

"Total recall," said Billy, admiringly. "Better get a toasted cheese and tomato on sourdough to go, too. Thanks, man." He turned to her again. "You sure you don't want something to eat?"

She shook her head.

While they waited for the two slices of bread to be crisped and browned, and the cheese to melt, she tried to figure out why this place intimidated her. *Too cool* sort of summarized it, but that meant what, exactly? The interior: expensively minimalist design. The staff: black wraparound aprons, defined biceps, hipster ink and piercings. And the clientele: Lululemon-ed, with high Wi-Fi expectations.

Then there was the absence of a visible price list. The chalk-board had a range of food and drinks written in arty, spiky script—no prices. The printed menus had prices, but by the time you asked for one of those, you were committed to buying something, weren't you? Or could you just browse the menu, register that a toasted cheese and tomato was going to cost you twelve bucks to go and sixteen to eat in, and back out of there, slowly? How much better was it going to be than the toasted cheese and tomato on Albert Street for less than half the price? Or the one you could make yourself, after school, for about a twentieth of the price? Billy paid and they left.

She looked at him, happily eating and walking, and decided it was unlikely that he had ever, even once in his life, had to make that kind of calculation. Whereas her life was full of those little lists of impossible figures—how hourly pay rates would add up to a new lens or more prints for her portfolio or a return airfare to Sydney or winter boots or Chanel instead of a cheap brand of nail polish (once, just once).

Billy had finished the coffee and sandwich by the time they got to the common room. He dumped his rubbish into the bin.

"What are you calling that meal?"

"A post-breakfast, pre-recess snack, I guess," he said, burping. "Sorry, that's gross. I think I know how we're going to get this up." He walked over to the camera zone and pulled a table right up underneath the corner of the ceiling to which it was fixed. He put a chair on the table and balanced a stool on the chair. He then put another chair on the table next to it. He jumped down and went to the cupboard in the kitchen area where he'd stashed a tripod with telescopic legs.

"Did you nick that from the art room?"

"Borrowed it," he said.

"Did you sign it out?"

"Nuh."

"Then you nicked it."

"But isn't nicking something for a defined and finite time pretty similar to borrowing?"

"Similar, except in the detail of the owners not knowing where it is or who's got it."

Billy smiled. "They're always telling us that the student body *is* the school, so if I *am* the school, don't *I* sort of own it?"

Michael walked in to hear her ask, "Won't they see us? Like, now? On the screens?" As she spoke, she carefully placed herself out of viewing range, kicking herself that she hadn't thought of it earlier.

"The full-time security dude doesn't get in till eight. I can't imagine them looking at earlier footage unless there'd been some sort of break-in overnight."

Billy gave Michael a cool look. "Hey, man—you're turning up a lot, lately. Are you actually following us? Or is this just a whole lot of bad luck?"

Michael put his bag down. "In this case, I am following you."

"Just so you know, it's creepy."

Vân Ước gave Michael an apologetic shrug as Billy got a folder out of his bag, and from the folder a print of the photo Vân Ước had helped him shoot of the empty room, which he'd stuck onto a piece of cardboard, so it was rigid.

He got a roll of tape out, made some tape loops, and stuck the print on the plate of the tripod where a camera usually went.

"Okay." He climbed up on the table, and onto the chair on

the table, then pulled out the tripod legs to their maximum length and positioned them so they'd fit on the stool. He maneuvered the tripod until the photographic image was close to the camera on the ceiling.

"What do you think?" he asked Vân Ước.

"Should be about right."

"Why are you getting Vân Ước involved in this?" Michael asked. "She could get into trouble purely at the service of your weak joke."

"Yeah, only she has this thing—free will?" said Billy.

"If you expect this to work, you'll have to go and check that the photo edges are out of shot on the security screen," said Michael. "And you also have to know you will definitely get caught within a couple of days, and Vân Ước can't afford to be part of that."

Billy climbed down carefully, so as not to move the chair/stool/tripod assemblage. "Okay, now can you go?"

Michael ignored Billy and said to Vân Ước, "It's not a smart idea for you to be involved. Think about it."

She was already involved. "Billy said he'll take the blame."

"That's not always the perpetrator's call, unfortunately," said Michael.

Billy pulled a Sharpie from his bag and wrote a note— DON'T MESS WITH THIS—IT'S SHOWING THE COMMON ROOM EMPTY ON THE SECURITY CAMERA. YOU'RE WELCOME—and taped it conspicuously in front of the chair/stool/tripod tower.

A few people were starting to straggle in.

"What's that meant to be? Art?" asked Annie suspiciously,

looking at the setup. But on reading the sign, she was thrilled. "Classic, Billy. Classic."

Billy headed off to training, late again, and Vân Ước to rehearsal.

● ● ●

By morning break everyone knew that the rebels had taken the common room, and people were freely lighting up cigarettes in there—"Just like the good old days," as Pippa said, blowing smoke out the window with a dreamy *all's right with the world* smile.

Billy had a look at the security screens on a bogus visit to lost property and reported that it looked completely realistic. An innocently empty room was all that appeared on the screen.

More deceptive appearances.

And Michael, of course, was right; being part of a popular funny-boy prank involved more anxiety than fun.

34

They stood at the edge of the sandpit together at homework club that Friday in a harmonious lull. Nobody was hitting anybody or attempting to take the implement that someone else was using. Vardi was scratching her head again. More lice. Vân Ước would have to remind Vardi's mother about the importance of getting rid of the eggs, not just the critters, and give her another information sheet. Vân Ước probably should have taken her out of the sandpit, but, seriously, it was a losing battle in this age group. Someone was always scratching.

"I've been thinking about rowing—you know, what you were asking me about why I like it," said Billy.

"And?"

"I guess I pretty much accepted the family assumption that I'd do it, like it, and be good at it."

"They assumed right, didn't they?"

"I don't know. I've been imagining what it would be like to step away."

She remembered the vaunting pride of Billy's father at the after-regatta party, the *row, Crowthorne, row* hoo-ha. "Your father would probably have a heart attack."

"I guess." Billy didn't look too perturbed at the idea.

"You've only got two more seasons to get through."

"Not really." His tone was wry, but he looked tired. "The commitment and work and early mornings and ergos in the pain cave and a coach yelling at me to be better will continue in America."

"True."

"Whereas some people might enjoy taking a year off after school. A year away from timetables and up at dawn and pain."

"What might those people do?"

Billy smiled. "They might bum around for a while doing whatever the fuck they want. Like nothing much. Those people might even get to sleep in."

"And that sounds good?"

"Oh yeah." He'd obviously been mulling this over. "It's starting to feel... like a straightjacket."

She listened, throwing an *I can see what you're up to* look at Sam, who was getting a bit feisty with the digging in the sandpit.

"Like I've been this *thing* for my family, for the school, but maybe I don't want that anymore."

"Wow. Has anyone ever quit the first eight, evereverever? Isn't it like abdicating the sports crown?"

"Yeah. Only it's such bullshit. I mean, sure, I'd feel bad for my crew, but there's at least four guys in the seconds who'd kill for a place in the firsts and do a fantastic job."

"Are you serious, or is this one of your rebellious-boy-behaves-badly stunts?"

"You disapprove of me still, I see."

"Jesus."

"Jesus yourself. I've never heard you swear before."

"I've never heard you quote *Jane Eyre* before."

They looked at each other.

"This feels…real," he said.

"It can't be, can it? You didn't know I existed until a few weeks ago."

"We've known each other forever, haven't we?"

Those words rang so true and untrue. Her response to them sprang from her well-stocked imagination as much as her keenly awakened body. She felt the tangle of sex and longing and fairy tales with handsome boys and happy endings. She was peering into the well, ready to tumble in, and what then? These stories with enchantments and wishes weren't her stories. She was smarter than that. She was nobody's Cinderella. She wasn't going to fall for this *we've known each other forever*, was she?

Had she?

Had they?

How disconcerting it was to have an idle fantasy turn into real-life attraction.

• • •

If she could find a way of reversing the wish, of leaving the seductive land of possible false pretenses, she had to take it. Urgent priority. No doubt, she was going to miss the adoring gaze of Billy Gardiner. But you couldn't build something real on such a shaky foundation. If this *were* tricked-up, pretendo love, the day the wish dissolved, or passed its use-by date, would be a disaster.

Imagine Billy looking at her in the cold light of day and knowing—or would he even remember?—she'd been having her way with him. Using him for her own pleasure and amusement. It made her blush. And what would school be like once the spell was broken? Relegated to the invisible realm once more. All his friends so relieved that he had finally come to his senses. What had he been thinking? Did that really happen?

What, in fact, was happening?

Free writing time-out.

> *Billy is attracted to me because I wished he would be (using a magical wish vial, from a creative writing prompts box). I wished that he found me attractive above all others and…fascinating. (Embarrassing to even write it down. Cannot be true.)*
>
> *First theory still right: Billy Gardiner is perpetrating the longest, most believable, most utterly plausible setup of a joke in the history of the world. (Surely unlikely that he could fake all that kissing with unequivocal physical responses to being close to me—e.g., erect penis, fast breathing, soft moaning. Or is this something I don't*

understand about male sexual response?? Does not discriminate between true love and potential joke victim? Loath to believe that.)

OR: *Billy Gardiner started off intending to play a mean joke on me but changed his mind along the way and has fallen for me for real. (A little bit aww, but mostly problematic: Could I love someone who set out with the intention of being mean to me? Needs more thought + possible consult w Jess.)*

OR: *This is dream life, and I will wake up in the morning back in real life. (Sign of current level of confusion that this one is shaping up as possible frontrunner.)*

OR: *Billy suddenly noticed me, and fell for me, for no particular reason. (But surely unmotivated blitz love happens at first sight or not at all [more likely the latter].)*

OR: *Unbeknownst to his conscious mind, Billy had unconsciously been aware of me for a longer time than he realized (e.g., he knew about my academic results from last year???).*

Hope hard drive can't remember/tell anyone/send a message to my whole e-mail contact list that I wrote "erect penis." (That's twice, now.) Jess would think nothing of writing "erect penis." (Three times.) Though as a lesbian-in-waiting, she is perhaps less likely to have cause to write it. Why am I such an idiot? No good answer to that.

Select All. Delete.

35

A Friday movie with Jess had been the weekly high point of Vân Ước's life for a long time. The tradition started because their year-six teacher, Ms. Clegg, had been worried about the parents putting too much pressure on the girls in the run-up to high school entrance exams. She took the trouble to write a letter and get it translated. The thrust of the letter was that the girls needed leisure time as well as study time, that it could be instructive and help their English study. She knew the way to the mothers' hearts. An example she used was the selection of suitable DVDs, which could also help the girls understand popular culture and improve their idiomatic English.

Ever since that fateful letter, the Friday movie had been acceptable to the mothers, as much as music practice or math or French grammar. They'd come to think of it as actual homework. And it coincided with Vân Ước's parents' regular dinner with her dad's cousin in Footscray, to which Bác Bảo was also invited, and from which Vân Ước, the only kid, was excused.

Thank god for Ms. Clegg. They'd started off with anthology packs that Jess's mother sourced from who knew where, such as *Classic American TV Shows of the 70s*, *Sitcom Medley*, *Favorite Hollywood Musicals*, etc., but had long ago graduated to whatever they wanted to watch.

Mind you, the *Favorite Hollywood Musicals* boxed set had prompted many hilarious nights teaching themselves to tapdance, an adaptable life skill. And even though dance scenes from *Pulp Fiction* and *(500) Days of Summer* had replaced those from early musicals as their favorites, films like *Singin' in the Rain* would always rate highly with them.

● ● ●

Jess was able to report back favorably on Billy from the afternoon's encounter at homework club.

"Okay, he came and found me—I was upstairs, so good effort. He called me Jessica, making eye contact."

"You sound like a private investigator."

"I *was* investigating him—assessing his suitability as a possible boyf for my bestie."

"He seems to have been reading *Jane Eyre*, too."

"Check. He is stuck in the quagmire of Jane's stay with the Rivers family."

221

"Understandable. It does get very religious there."

"Some, including me, would say boring. But it's also a good two-thirds of the way in, so he's put some time into it since last week."

"True."

"He's passed my tests and I can only confirm that my original diagnosis was correct. He is besotted."

"For whatever reason," Vân Ước said darkly.

"You are lovable, whatever you choose to think. And he can't help it that he comes from the right side of the tracks."

● ● ●

At the mid-movie food break, she told Jess about the L-word conversation.

"*Despite your beauty being…great…it's the least of the reasons I love you…* Those were his exact words?"

"Yeah. He may have been like three-quarters flippant."

"But he didn't take them back? Or make a joke of it?"

"No, he seemed surprised to hear himself say it. He said, *I've never said that before.*"

"That sounds more like three-quarters serious. Or even four-quarters."

"Or like someone who is under an influence he can't control."

Jess held up her hand. "No crazy talk on film night."

While they assembled their food, Vân Ước also divulged the physical status of the Billy relationship.

"You let him flick the bean?" Jess nearly choked on her mini-frankfurter in a bun with jalapeño sauce and coleslaw.

Vân Ước was breaking up the family-size block of Snack chocolate, feeling dreamy as she remembered. "I would not have thought I could—you know—with someone, but it was like we were under a spell. I've done it so many times with imaginary Billy, it was kind of weird to actually have him there in real life."

Jess rolled her eyes. "Is it time for our visit to a faraway land to buy you some condoms?"

"Nope. That's it for now. At least till I sort out what's going on."

"What's going *on*? You've committed school crime with the guy. Which I still think is dumb. He's stood up for you in public against former friends of his, like horrible Holly and tedious Tiff. You're going *out*. And he explicitly asked you. He *loves* you, and not just for your looks. And he said those words, too. You let him flick—"

"Hey, you were totally against him until this afternoon."

"It's called an about-face. He was a probable arrogant twat who, surprisingly, has proved himself to be a possibly worthy mew for you."

"And you know what I mean. Sort *it* out. IT. The wish. I've got that writer's address. I'm going over there tomorrow. I hope I'll have the guts to knock on her door."

"Be serious, what could you possibly say to her?"

"I know."

"But say that first thing was a wish, and you got another wish, you would just take a moment and think carefully about how you phrase it, wouldn't you? You know that whole 'be careful what you wish for' thing?"

"Yeah."

"It's a thing for a reason."

"Of course I'd be careful."

"Okay, good, but seeing as how in real life there isn't a wish on the horizon, the only things you really need to sort out are (1) how you feel about him, and (2) if it's serious, how you can hide it from your parents."

Jess hit PLAY but Vân Ước was only half tuning in to the film. It would be tricky phrasing a re-wish. She ran through some options:

I wish Billy just liked me to an appropriate extent.

(Appropriate according to whom?)

I wish Billy liked me as a friend, and let's see where that takes us.

(Not bad. But what if it took them nowhere?)

I wish Billy loved me for all time.

(No. What if she only had Billy-love maximum capacity of a few months?)

I wish Billy believed we were destined to be together.

(See above.)

I wish Billy liked me the same amount he did before that creative writing class.

(That was not at all. And, it wasn't much fun.)

I wish Billy thought he'd like to get to know me better.

(Tepid.)

I wish Billy wanted to get to know me really well, and that would lead to love.

(Better. But what would the perimeter of this love be? Time frame, extent, exact nature of the love, etc.)

I wish Billy only had eyes for me.

(Could risk falling over and injuring himself or others. Unappealing, narrow worldview.)

I wish Billy loved me.

(Could be caught out in a past tense technicality: *loved*, not *loves*?)

I wish Billy liked me, in real life, to the same extent that he likes me now, but not because of a wish.

(Could be like a double negative equivalent to wish for an outcome that was not the result of a wish.)

Hmmm, she'd slipped into the realm of "better wish," rather than "negate the wish," too. More work needed.

36

Twelve Balmain Street, Abbotsford. This had to be her house—assuming that the one listed *R. Bartloch* in the directory was the writer who'd given the creative writing master class. The shutters were shut. She could see some fresh junk mail in the letterbox, despite the ADDRESSED MATERIAL ONLY sign. A Tibetan prayer flag, fraying and fading, flapped in the breeze, and a collection of china birds was visible inside on the left-hand front window ledge. A flowerbed alongside the gappy, paling fence sported some alarmingly tall, large-faced sunflowers in full, fake-looking but real, bloom. All these things fitted very neatly into the realm of domestic accessories she imagined would be favored by a pink-haired, witchy-booted, retro-sundressed, shoebox-toting, possible-wish-trouble-causing writer.

Vân Ước was relieved to see that the house looked unoccupied. Wimp that she was, it was the only thing that allowed her to walk up the weed-lined path to the front door and knock. No answer. Phew.

Well, what a pathetic waste of effort—and why bother knocking? It was as though part of her brain really did believe that the old dudes saw everything. *Credit where credit's due: She marched right up to the front door and knocked very firmly/Only because she was sure no one was home/But at least she stopped herself from looking like a random lurking fool—in the event that any of the neighbors were peering from their windows/Of course there were neighbors peering from their windows—what else are neighbors on a quiet street going to be doing at 10 a.m. on a Saturday?/In that case she acquitted herself well, eyes to the front, good posture, minimum street loitering and, by gee, she made a quick getaway/And the big question is, will she front up again next Saturday?/Only time will tell…*

37

Home after work, she walked in to find her mother in the living room, on the sofa, hands folded, looking grim. Her group therapy session—or friendship circle, as they called it—had finished half an hour ago. Usually at this time, Vân Ước could rely on having the place to herself, knowing that her mother and father and Bác Bảo would be over at the Footscray market getting the week's food and not back for at least another hour and a half; they went late for the bargains.

"Hey, Mama." Vân Ước sat down next to her. "Are you okay? How come you're not with Dad? How was friendship circle?"

"Today we were talking all about when we were children."

Why couldn't she just ask her mother about the photo? Ask

her why they never saw her aunt? Now, right now, would be a perfect time. Only she felt like such a snoop.

"So, talking about when you were a kid—that made you... how'd that make you feel?" What to do? Did her mother need her hand held?

No, her mother took her hand away and put it back in her lap. It was clear that she was feeling uncomfortable. She was visibly composing herself, folding herself back together, straightening out the raggedy edges, smoothing hair away from her face. "It was hard for me to talk about my mother. Thinking of times in my life I have wanted her and have not had that comfort."

"Can I make you some tea?"

"Thank you, Vân Ước, *con*. Tea would be nice."

Vân Ước put the kettle on and prepared tea. Through all her mother's past struggles with the effects of post-traumatic stress disorder, she had never spoken of how she was feeling, never given voice to her vulnerability. Her more typical mode was simply to disappear into the bedroom. So was this a good or a bad thing? She imagined that some freeing up of feelings following group therapy was perfectly normal.

"Can you tell me some of the things you talked about?"

"Her cooking. We had a small area to prepare food, but it was always so fresh and delicious."

"Like when you cooked at the hostel?"

"Yes. And we all got into such trouble, but I could still make a good meal over the little radiator if I had to."

Her parents had told her of their time living in the hostel in

Moreland. The food there sounded like bulk-order, cheap cafeteria fare, not at all suited to their tastes or diet or digestive systems. When new people arrived at the hostel, they went eagerly to the canteen for free food, but numbers dropped off sharply after each new wave tried the food there.

So people bought pots and small bar radiators at the local secondhand store and cooked in their bedrooms, using the radiators lying on their backs as hot plates. A pan, some noodles or rice, a few vegetables, some fish, some chili, lemongrass. One family would cook rice, another family vegetables, and they would share the meal. They constantly got into trouble with the hostel management, who claimed they were creating hygiene and fire hazards and confiscated all the cooking implements. They were easy to repurchase. In this haven—a bed, a door that locked, a toilet that flushed, clean water flowing from the taps—it had seemed so strange to her parents that someone should be angry with them simply because they wanted to cook dinner.

The kitchen in their home now was more than adequate for all the cooking they did as a family, and Vân Ước smiled to think what her parents would make of a kitchen like the one in Billy's house.

Her mother stood up. "I will wash my face and make some lunch."

"I'll help."

Her mother hesitated. "It wasn't only me, but many of us in the friendship circle, who didn't see our parents again after we left. It was like having to choose between our parents and our children." Vân Ước felt her mother's hand on her shoulder, as light as a little bird. "Even the ones we didn't have yet."

Her mother had never shared anything like this with her before. Never expressed such emotion. The understanding that she wasn't alone in her sadness and disappointments must be soothing. The permission—encouragement—to open up and share after all these years must be like finding a new room in a house you thought you knew.

"You know you can talk to me any time you want?" Vân Ước willed herself to mention the photo, but failed once again.

"Enough talking." Her mother stood up. The conversation was over.

Vân Ước snipped some coriander from the pots on the kitchen windowsill, turned on the tap to fill the sink with cold water, and went to the fridge to get out some vegetables. It was Saturday: they'd be making a use-the-leftover-vegetables soup or omelet before her father and Bác Bảo returned from the market with fresh supplies.

38

Jess was right. Vân Ước had been so busy guessing what cogs were turning in Billy's brain, she had not spent enough time sorting out how she felt herself.

A free writing scrutiny of Where My Heart's Been At. By me. Year Eleven.

1

 It started with a distant infatuation. Billy Gardiner—have always thought of him like that: Billy Gardiner—like Jordan Catalano, Tim Riggins, Jonah Griggs. Some boys, fictional and real-life, seem to warrant both names. It felt as unreal as any celebrity crush. Nothing would come of it.

2

Despite that conviction, the infatuation grew. Desire grew. Ultimate mew! And there he was right under my nose. Every day.

Complicating factor: Not admirable! White-boy beauty fetishizing. Bad girl, Vân Ước. (Also: he has not always acted like the nicest person in the world.)

3

Though I've always found him to be a bit more nuanced and mysterious than he gets credit for being.

4

When he was following me around and I was convinced he was up to no good, I actively went off him. He was annoying. And he stuck like glue. I felt genuine irritation to see him looking down at me over the bathroom stall wall.

5

So, now I am convinced he likes me. Therefore it follows that I should be—happy? Even if his affection turns out to be wish-induced?

6

Interesting side note: It certainly hasn't delivered the one thing I thought would be a part of going out with Billy: peer approval. Although it's made me realize that I probably already had a level of approval from people I like, whose opinions I do value, e.g., Lou, Michael, Sibylla.

7

So what do I feel? Heart, speak me some truth.

Infatuation, though that is transforming into something

more like—*affection. I real-life like Billy. And he has truly gone from being Billy Gardiner to being Billy. Physical attraction (to the max) (worse than before). Ego balm, yes, unavoidable—he does look like a god. Love. (?). Curiosity. Tick. Confusion. Tick. Tick.*

What would Jane do?

Jane, what would you do?

Jane would be honest. Up-front. She'd look at the situation here and possibly say that she did not perceive a problem. She—who had to contend with the wedding-day revelation of the existence of her beloved Rochester's insane wife, and resist a tempting offer to throw doubt to the winds and run off with said beloved, flouting all Victorian ideals of propriety and piety—might well think, pfffft, what is your problem, Vân Ước? Are you a woman or a wimp?

8

Impediments to my relationship with Billy:

The wish-wondering. Major problem. Am possibly living a massive lie.

I'm not allowed to date anyone.

His parents' almost-certain disapproval of me.

His friends' certain disapproval of me.

So.

Can't change my parents' rules.

Can't change what people think.

Have to deal with the wish.

Select All. Delete.

What to do?

Jane had all the answers. Of course she did. When had she ever let Vân Ước down? It struck her like a proverbial bolt from the blue that within *Jane Eyre*'s framework of realism—of social commentary on class, on charity schools, on imperious rich relations, on gender equality and the restricted opportunity for women, on love and morality...there was also some mad magic.

She went to her desk and sat down. The more she flicked through the familiar pages, the more fragments of magic appeared everywhere. Jane believes the moon had spoken to her. Jane feels foreboding that the chestnut tree had been split asunder in a storm. Jane believes in presentiments, sympathies, and signs. She has unsettling repeated dreams of a baby. But where was the passage she was looking for...?

It was one of her favorite parts of the book, because on first encounter she'd been so afraid (reading breathlessly, terrified) that St. John Rivers, through sheer zealous, insistent power, would persuade Jane into a loveless marriage of duty as a missionary in a distant land where she'd contract cholera and die.

Aha—here it was. Jane hears her name called three times:

...it did not seem in the room—nor in the house—nor in the garden: it did not come out of the air—nor from under the earth—nor from overhead. I had heard it—where, or whence, forever impossible to know! And it was the voice of a human being—a known, loved, well-remembered voice—that of Edward Fairfax Rochester; and it spoke in pain and woe wildly, eerily, urgently.

It felt so real. Yet it couldn't have been, surely? But Jane, sensible Jane, Jane who would sit down in a kitchen and prepare gooseberries for a pie, had believed the unbelievable.

"Down superstition!" I commented, as that specter rose up black by the black yew at the gate. "This is not thy deception, nor thy witchcraft: it is the work of nature. She was roused, and did—no miracle—but her best."

Nature roused, and doing her best. Huh. So the cosmos took care of things?

Vân Ước sighed. That did not feel like a digital-age solution.

39

There was something distinctive about the door buzzer: it never buzzed without them knowing in advance who was buzzing. It would be Bác Bảo on Saturday. If it was Vân Ước or her parents without their key—rare—they would tap on the security grille and call out. If it was Jess or her mum, they'd do the same. So when the buzzer buzzed at 6 p.m. on Saturday, the three of them froze.

"Who is it?" her mother asked—not into the buzzer intercom, just into the room.

Vân Ước leapt to her feet. What if...It couldn't be Billy, could it? He would know the apartment number from the class list. But surely he'd call before buzzing.

She hurried across to the intercom. He must not be accidentally clicked through. She wasn't ready to show herself to Billy quite this close up and personal. Not yet.

"Hello?"

"Hey. Is this a bad time?"

"Kinda."

"Can I come up for a few minutes?"

"Wait there—I'll come down."

She neutralized her expression, took a deep breath, and turned to face her parents.

"It's the tall friend of Eleanor's. Billy. From school."

"What does he want?" her father asked. He'd been in a comfortable nod over the newspaper before the buzz.

Her mother jumped up and started clearing things away. "He wants to come up here?"

Eleanor visited once a year; it was always an occasion for pride—generous hospitality, way too much food preparation and a little anxiety.

"No! No—it's for our English homework. He just wants me to go over one thing with him."

"Why not do it over the phone?"

"You're right." She rolled her eyes and nodded, hoping it looked convincing.

Both her parents were clearly thrown by this unscheduled intrusion.

She ducked into her bedroom and picked up her copy of *Ariel*. "I'll be ten minutes."

They were not convinced.

"It's still light outside. We'll be in the garden."

"Take your phone," her mother said.

• • •

She headed down in the elevator, which had been renovated not so long ago, lined in fashionable patterned stainless-steel sheeting, but had by now been defaced and thoroughly scratched up and written on. Shame. She swiped her bangs across with one hand and straightened her back. She'd just eaten an apple, so her breath should be fine. Like Jane, she didn't really have much in the way of finery—*I had no article of attire that was not made with extreme simplicity*...It was a jeans and T-shirt day, as usual. She smoothed down her T-shirt.

The elevator picked up on eight, six, and three, and finally, with a ping and a shudder, they hit the ground floor.

She stepped out last and walked through the heavy security door to Billy, leaning against the wall on the other side.

She smiled at the front desk guy, Ralph, on her way out. He was her favorite night-shift guy.

"Your doorman looks like a bit of a Rottweiler," Billy said as they walked into the mild evening.

"He's got to protect innocent tenants from people like you."

"He was extremely suspicious. I waved for him to let me in, but no-go."

"He probably thought you were a debt collector or a process server."

"What are the people who live here like?"

"Like me."

"And?"

"Well, it's low-income housing, so there are old poor people, young poor people, families of poor people. Take your pick."

"But is it, like, transitional, or do people stay?"

"Both."

"How long have you been here?"

"My parents have been here for thirty years. They won't leave."

"Will you ever invite me up?"

"Maybe." Maybe not.

"That must be some view from the twelfth floor."

"It is. So, why are you here?"

"Where can we sit?"

Vân Ước led them to the empty playground. The site of her own play, as a child. The site of many boring hours babysitting kids from the apartments. The site of stupid behavior of the boys she knew from primary school. And now the site of side-by-side swings, with Billy. Oh, life.

He leaned way back, holding the swing chains and closing his eyes. "Man, that still feels like being a kid."

She remembered—there'd been another big regatta on this afternoon, while she was busy at work, rolling rolls.

"How'd you go today?"

"We won. Too easy." He groaned and sat back up straight.

"That's a lie. I'm totally wrecked. And I split some blisters. My own fault; I should've toughened my skin up more." He held up a bandaged hand and she had to stop herself from picking it up and kissing it better.

"You could be home, resting in the lap of. What are you doing here in the tanbark?"

"Seeing you."

"Where do your parents think you are?"

"At Ben's. I'll go there in a while. You're invited, if you want to come."

"I'm only allowed out in *exceptional* circumstances."

"How come you could go to mine last weekend?"

"I pitched it to my parents as an official school community celebration of a rowing victory event."

Billy laughed. "It's just a tweak, I guess."

They swung in silence. The mild air smelled like autumn and damp and tanbark with the background whiff of hundreds of kitchen exhaust fans.

Even without the troubling existence of the wish question mark, how would they ever be able to go out? How far could she push her parents? How far could Billy push his? How could she ever fit in at all these social gatherings that happened, invisibly funded by parents? How could she even take the time out from study for them?

He obviously had mind-reading skills. "The girls—they're not as smart as you, but they're not so bad when you get to know them. Except Holly, maybe."

"You've obviously changed your mind about her."

"I guess everyone's allowed to make the occasional inebriated mistake."

"True. I just wish you'd made it with someone else."

"Me too. Hey, I finished *Jane Eyre*."

"And?"

"Yeah, it's cool. I can see why it's stayed in print for a hundred and sixty-seven years." He reached over and pushed her off course so she was swinging in a half twist and had to stop. "Tell me why you like it so much."

"I love Jane."

"Because..."

"She has no ostensible power, but she is powerful. She's inconspicuous—modest and unprepossessing—but her presence is strong. She stands up to injustice. She has self-respect. She isn't afraid to speak plainly about her feelings. She is so passionate, despite all the restrictions and confinement of her background. She's generous. And she's an artist."

Billy looked at her in his assessing way. "It's the *Vân Ước as English teacher* making a rare but persuasive appearance."

She smiled. "Do I sound like an idiot?"

"I just like it when you talk. You're so quiet most of the time."

"No surprise I like the quiet girls' hero."

His eyes lit up.

"Not you. Jane."

"Oh." He reached over and touched her face, stood up, pulled her up from the swing, and kissed her like he really meant it.

She broke away with a sigh. "We can't do this here." She

turned him to face the building. "See all those windows? Potential informants, the lot of them."

"But one day...we'll get to go out on a date and kiss all we want."

She smiled. "Date night. The final frontier."

40

The trouble with the photo in the common room/security camera scam—apart from the fact that someone was bound to wake up to it pretty soon—was that the whole tripod/stool assemblage had to be taken down every afternoon and set up again every morning. Because of the cleaners. It was lucky they'd made it through Thursday and Friday without getting caught.

When Billy breezed in and started gathering the apparatus to set up the camera early on Monday morning, Ben had other ideas. "Can you get Vince to do that?"

"I can do it," Billy said.

"Don't be an idiot," Ben said, sounding as pissed off as he ever sounded, which was still quite controlled. "It's four weeks. Are you *trying* to fuck up?"

"Oh, right. Okay—Vince, buddy, can you rig it up?"

"Sure." Vince clambered up on the table and chair and fiddled around setting the tripod up.

At Vân Ước's questioning look, Billy explained, "Head of the River, four weeks away."

Ben smiled, now that he'd got his way, and added, "He's no good to us with a broken collarbone or a sprained wrist."

Vince feigned an elaborate wobble and almost-fall—which turned into a real almost-fall, accompanied by loud expletives as he regained his balance just in time.

"I can't believe it's so soon," said Billy.

"And victory will be ours," said Ben.

"If you say so, my brother," Billy said.

Once again, the barely contained, pissed-off look flickered in Ben's eyes; it encompassed Vân Ước as well as Billy. He headed out of the common room, pausing at the door with a smile. "I say so. And make sure you fix your hand. Get some alcohol on it."

Billy gave a lazy salute to the empty doorway.

41

Ms. Norton was giving her a quizzical look at the end of her orals practice session. Vân Ước felt as though she hadn't breathed properly, had spoken too fervently, and had poured out with concentration all the love she felt for Sylvia Plath's work.

"Too much?" she asked, taking a deep breath.

"Vân Ước Phan—could you please start speaking in class?"

She felt a flood of relief that this new assessment form was going to be okay.

"Tell me, how many times might you have read 'Daddy'?"

She tried to estimate. "Perhaps twenty, thirty times? Maybe a few more."

"Your responses are original and well expressed. You obviously thought about the poems, and had plenty of your own ideas, before you did the critical reading—and that, in my book, is the perfect way to read poetry. Well done."

"Thank you. She's about my favorite poet."

"I think you've infected your study partner with a bit of enthusiasm, too."

"We talked a lot—about her."

"Good work on all counts, then. I'm going to tell you what I tell all my strong students—remember your work/life balance. The time you've put into this shows, and it's to your credit. But do schedule some downtime."

"I will. Thank you, Ms. Norton." She took her soft-with-wear copy of *Ariel* and left, heading for a portfolio meeting with Ms. Halabi.

Work/life balance? She didn't even have life/life balance. It was more than she could cope with just trying to balance the wildly veering versions of real life versus wish life.

● ● ●

Her new portfolio idea was a composite of close-ups of the perfect turf that blanketed the main oval. It seemed to be subject to intense attention; someone was always pulling out a weed, aerating the soil, measuring the moisture levels. It was a super-green graphic dream. She'd done some test shots of the grass at different angles and composed them in a grid that made the grass squares look like a woven textile.

Ms. Halabi looked through the prints and the rough composited image. "Talk to me."

"Well, it's another example, I suppose, of focusing on a little thing—blades of grass, we walk on them, we don't notice them particularly…"

"And what it means to you…?"

"It's beautiful, if you look."

Ms. Halabi was nodding. "There's no doubt that you can present a portfolio and pretty much just say that—*It's a fresh look at the small things. It's easy to overlook what is right before our eyes or under our feet*—but the examiners are fond of a narrative. That's why I keep asking."

"I don't really have one."

"Yet. There's no desperate hurry. We're in a two-year program. I'm going to keep asking, though."

"Okay."

"Lovely work. But keep it in the back of your mind: What does it mean? What does it mean *to you*?"

42

She'd never much asked the second of Ms. Halabi's questions. Always looking for meaning, deciphering codes, sure—how to present, how to study, how to fit in, how to disappear, how to fake it—but never enough *what does it mean to me?* She was used to second-guessing, staying in the background, and waiting for real life to begin in some distant future.

If the thing with Billy was going to happen—if—she was never going to be friends with the girls in his group. Pippa might be an exception; she showed occasional signs of being human, at least.

But Vân Ước had never tried to make her own friends here, never initiated any friendly contact. It wasn't on the list. She could walk to practice with Polly, sit in a class meeting next to Lou, and talk about irrational and transcendental numbers with Michael, but she'd pretty much thought of these years as the study zone, and imagined that real life—life as an art student, life with friends and lovers—would magically start when school finished. Art school was where she'd meet her people.

But maybe life couldn't be kept incubating indefinitely. Maybe it was ready to hatch a bit earlier, like right now, if only she'd play along.

She took the winged cardigan out of her bag. This clear, bright Tuesday, the first day of autumn, was the day to set it free, let it find its next custodian. She hadn't had a chance to wear it again anywhere special, but she'd enjoyed living with this thing of strange beauty. She'd wondered a thousand times about its maker, its history, and its future. It was folded and tied up with a ribbon. The tag never had turned up, so she'd made a new one and pinned it inside, to make sure the cardigan's story continued.

"I spy stolen goods," said Holly when she saw the parcel.

"Lock up your valuables, people," said Ava.

Lou was bent down tying her sneakers. She stood up and faced them—a formidable, bespectacled avenging angel. She had a big voice when she wanted to use it. Secret singer's projection knowledge, no doubt.

"Do you understand that what you just said is basically illegal? That it's defamatory to slur somebody by lying about them? That you are, potentially, damaging Vân Ước's reputation 'in the eyes of reasonable people,' which is the legal test for defamation? That if she decided to sue you and you were prosecuted, you'd be ordered to pay her damages? *Do you?* Do you realize that?"

"Settle down. If she gives it back, no biggie, right?" said Holly.

"SHE DIDN'T STEAL IT."

"Fine. Have it your way. Freak. But we all know the truth. As if any garment has ever had a tag that says WEAR ME."

Michael looked up from his notebook.

"Are you looking at me?" Holly asked.

"Yes," he said calmly.

"Well, don't." Holly and Ava walked out rolling their eyes and giving each other *crazy people* looks.

Michael had one of his abstracted whirring-cogs faces; it typically happened when he'd had a brain wave of some sort— a frequent occurrence. He looked around as though taking inventory of who was there—only about six people—shoved his notebook in his pack, and walked out.

Vân Ước braved up. She thought of balance. She thought, What does it mean *to me*? She thought of life being allowed to start here, right now, at school. She summoned her courage. "Lou—thank you for that."

Lou shook her head. "They're such idiots."

"I'm delivering the cardigan back into its habitat. Do you want to come for the walk?"

Lou smiled, as though she was genuinely pleased. Vân Ước corrected herself: Lou *was* genuinely pleased that she'd suggested they do something together, something friendly, something that had nothing to do with schoolwork.

They crossed the road and entered the Botanic Gardens. They walked in companionable silence for a while, until Vân

Ước remembered that this was officially her friend foray, so she should probably talk.

"What work do your parents do?" Okay, a bit random, but at least it was a start.

"One's a surgeon and the other's a history academic. What about your folks?"

"My mother does piecework sewing at home, mostly baby clothes. And my dad works in a chicken-processing plant."

"Wow. Hard work."

"Hard work, low wages. And if I get to do what I want to do, that'll make three of us."

Lou smiled. "Are you talking about art?"

"Yep. Only such a tiny percentage of artists make anything that resembles an income."

"True, but your stuff's awesome, so, who knows? Listen, do you mind me saying, you don't at all speak like someone whose parents have English as a second language."

"It's probably just from homework club."

"Really? Debi was your tutor, right? I sat near her last week—she's terrifying some poor kid with *Jane Eyre*."

"I was that poor kid five years ago. But it worked."

"As in…?"

"As in, I probably do sound like I come from an English-speaking family, I guess."

"Yeah, but *how* did it work? I'm tutoring now, don't forget; I need some tricks of the trade."

"For starters, I've got a totally warped work ethic—courtesy of my parents—and I just drilled vocab for years, like *really long lists* every single week. And paralleling that, I fell in love with reading. After *Jane Eyre* we read *Emma* and *Pride and Prejudice* and *Northanger Abbey* and *To Kill a Mockingbird* and *The Catcher in the Rye* and *Wuthering Heights* and *The Great Gatsby* and *Dubliners* and *Tess of the D'Urbervilles*—"

"Well, that one's a major downer," said Lou.

"Yes, I'm still recovering. And I've always read stacks of young adult fiction, and I like English as a subject and it all sank in, I guess. I suck at Vietnamese, though."

"Nobody's perfect."

"How did you know that legal stuff?"

Lou laughed. "TV."

"It was very convincing."

They arrived at the thatched shelter where Vân Ước had decided to leave the cardigan. It was on the opposite side of the gardens from where she'd found it. Maybe she should have gone farther afield, but she wanted somewhere a bit protected. She gave the parcel a kiss good-bye and put it gently on the seat inside the shelter.

"Farewell, pretty cardigan," said Lou.

They headed back in the direction of school.

Maybe this was a first step in her and Lou becoming proper friends. Jess could meet Lou and her mothers, and—she had a fleeting feeling of limitlessness, of disappearing boundaries, as she'd had at Mount Fairweather a couple of times—some days the horizon stretched right out.

It was a scary feeling for someone who'd lived a cautious life.

43

She got home that afternoon to find her mother crying.

Okay, a new level of expressing emotion could be good, right? Or had she unwittingly set in motion a flying-out-of-control/ mother-misery-increasing-forever thing?

"Mama, hi. Are you—can I get you anything?"

"No." Her mother plucked a rumpled tissue from the sleeve of her cardigan and blew her nose. "Maybe some water."

Vân Ước poured two glasses of cold water from the jug in the fridge and gave one to her mother.

"Anything you want to talk about?"

"Ha! It's all the talking that makes me cry. But they say it's 'normal,'" her mother said. "It's 'okay' to cry."

"Of course it's okay."

Her mother looked at her. "Listen to you—you are like a mother to me. Again." But her mother didn't sound happy about it; she looked fed up, actually.

Well, Vân Ước was fed up, too.

She'd always been comforted by how many words there were in the English language—more than a million. With so many words surely anything could be said, everything could be understood.

But what did the volume of words matter in any language when she couldn't even manage to ask the simplest questions? *Will you tell me your story? Will you let me into my own family? Isn't it my story, too?*

Enough!

She went into her parents' room and slipped the photo of the two small girls from under the paper lining in her mother's drawer. She brought it out and sat down with her mother. "I know I shouldn't have looked."

Her mother took the photo, sighed, and sipped the water. "It's me and Hoa Nhung."

"Please talk to me."

"I will start with a wish. When the boat landed…" Her mother nodded and paused, as though changing her mind.

Vân Ước held her breath. Even though her mother was skipping the whole chapter about what happened before they left Vietnam, and everything that might have happened during the journey itself, she was offering a fragment of her story. When the boat landed… Vân Ước was hungry, even for a morsel, just a crumb of story. She let maybe a minute pass. She could hear someone bumping around at Jess's. It would be Jess starting to get things ready for dinner.

"When the boat landed?" she prompted softly.

"It was a beach in Malaysia. We were taken by truck to the refugee camp."

"Who took you?"

"The army. Army officers. They gave us some food and water—just what they had with them."

"And the wish?"

"We spent a lot of time on the beach. It was so hot. But still, I walked up and down along the water's edge. And I was wishing. Wishing just one thing. Wishing that my arms could turn into wings—wide, strong wings with long, white feathers." Her mother's eyes were filling with tears again. Vân Ước patted her hand. Her mother wiped her eyes, smiling. "I never stopped wishing, but they didn't change into wings."

"Where did you want to go?"

"All I wanted was to fly across the sea, back to Vietnam, and be in my mother's arms again. I missed her so much. I couldn't bear to be parted from her."

"But you had to leave?"

"She wanted us to go. We knew it was our only hope for a life."

Vân Ước was scared to breathe, worried that she might break the talking spell. "I would miss you like that, Mama, if I had to leave."

Her mother gave her a tired smile. "No, *con*, not like that. My mother and I spoke the same language. You and I—our language is different."

Vân Ước felt guilty (again) that she'd dropped Vietnamese classes. But there wasn't time. It didn't have a role in her academic schedule, and that had to take priority. It was true her English was much better than her parents', and their Vietnamese was much better than hers, so they ended up communicating in the in-between zone of basic Vietnamese with a smattering of even more basic English, like three primary-school-aged children.

"I could go back and study more," she offered.

"It's not just language. It's…the whole culture."

Vân Ước knew the truth of that. How could she deny it, having felt the thousand injustices of her parents not understanding the life they had chosen for her?

"For my mother I had only respect and obedience. For her mother she had only respect and obedience…"

"I respect you, Ma."

"In the way that you can." Her mother nodded. "You're a good girl. But it is not the same. That chain has been broken. You have independence. *Ba* and I want that for you. But everything here is different. And that's still hard for me."

"But not *bad*?"

"No, not bad! You will have a good life. But the old life is gone forever."

Vân Ước felt the stab of a sad truth: she and her mother would never be as close as her mother and grandmother had been.

Her mother got up, stretched her tidy, graceful frame, and headed for the kitchen. Vân Ước wanted to be able to offer her some comfort, but what could she say? Her mother was right. The two of them represented an irreconcilable cultural split. Distance between them was inevitable.

"Thanks for talking to me," she said.

"Talking, huh! That's enough for now." Her mother pushed her hair back dismissively and straightened her cardigan. "Như Mai is always saying to the group, *Talk about your feelings, talk about your memories*. And now I am sad again. Because of all the talking! Off you go now. Time for homework."

But first Vân Ước wrapped her mother in a hug. In her usual prickly way—all shrug and elbow—Mama resisted initially, but relaxed for a moment and hugged back before patting Vân Ước's shoulder impatiently and pushing her gently in the direction of her room. "Study now!"

It only felt half as annoying as usual.

44

No more than ten minutes into lunchtime on Wednesday, Ms. King came into the year-eleven common room without knocking. It was raining outside, so the room was full. Pippa and Tiff flicked their cigarettes out the window and Holly swiped a saucer ashtray from a table in the kitchen area and dumped it in the bin.

"Get that down," Ms. King said, referring to the tripod-and-stool arrangement. "And gather round."

She wasn't looking amused.

"Would anyone like to start?" she asked. "Or do we treat you like year eights and say, *Nobody's leaving this room until someone confesses?*"

Billy was entirely unperturbed. "It was me," he said, sprawled on a sofa, with his mouth full.

Ms. King gave him the unblinking arctic stare she saved for very special occasions.

Billy swallowed, stood up, and repeated the sentence in a more formal manner. "It was me, Ms. King."

"And who are your henchmen?" She eyeballed a few of the guys she obviously considered to be the usual suspects.

Billy put up his hands, holding his wrists together. "Really, just me. Arrest me now. You didn't find it even a little bit amusing?"

"This is deceptive behavior, and we don't like it. It has led to further breaking of school rules, judging by the stench in here, and we don't like that. As well, it took security a few days to figure out what was going on, so now we look as though our systems don't work particularly well, and we don't like that, either. Who else is involved?"

Nobody said anything. Vân Ước wondered if she could swallow her fear and speak up. She was petrified by indecision. If the school decided to make a big deal out of this, it could jeopardize her scholarship. But despite Billy's offer to take the blame, she knew perfectly well what was required of her, because *what would Jane do?*

"Well? I've got all the time in the world," said Ms. King.

"As if Billy could take a photo to save his life," Holly muttered, staring at Vân Ước pointedly.

"Do you have something to say, Holly?"

"No, Ms. King."

"Ms. King," Vân Ước started. "I—"

Michael jumped to his feet and spoke over her. "Ms. King, I took the photograph."

Billy and Vân Ước and Ms. King all looked at him, surprised.

"Are you sure, Michael?" Ms. King asked.

Michael continued calmly, "I borrowed Vân Ước's camera, but she had no idea what I wanted to use it for."

She was touched by how quickly Michael—thinking all the time that the scheme was stupid and her involvement in it risky—had come to her defense once he realized she was about to speak up.

Ben Capaldi stormed into the common room, pouring rain and sweat, saying, "Billy, where the fuck were you?" before he registered Ms. King's presence and was also subjected to the snap-freeze gaze. "Apologies for the language, Ms. King," he said.

"Where was Billy Gardiner supposed to be?"

"We just had some lunchtime ergos; it's no big deal, we'll have another session after school."

"Well, immediately after school, he and Michael Cassidy will be in the principal's office with me, talking about appropriate discipline for this potentially dangerous prank," said Ms. King.

"How's it dangerous?" Billy asked, incredulous.

"You could have broken your neck setting it up. People have been smoking in here—which is a health risk that contravenes the school's clean air environment policy, and breaks the zero-tolerance smoking rule, and had there been a security problem with this room, no one would have known about it."

Billy's face showed his contempt.

Leaving the room with a final stern look at Billy and a puzzled one at Michael, Ms. King said, "Four thirty in Dr. Dryden's office, both of you."

"Big fucken deal," said Billy. "Seriously."

"You better not get kicked off the first eight," said Ben.

"Or what? You sound just like my dad," said Billy. He turned to Michael. "Thanks, man."

"It's for Vân Uớc, not you," said Michael.

"You should have told the truth," said Holly to Vân Uớc. "Dishonesty isn't nice. But I guess it's what you'd expect from a thief."

"Shut up, Holly," said Billy. "I told her not to. And stop saying she stole something."

Vân Uớc wanted to say, *I'm not a thief*, and, *I tried to speak up about the photos. I was prepared to own my part of the punishment.* But she said nothing.

She saw Michael's eyes flick over to Holly and glance around the room. He seemed satisfied to see it so crowded. He loathed bullies, and hypocrites, and Holly had clearly been in his sights ever since he'd been collateral damage in her betrayal of Sibylla. He put his book down, stood up, and cleared his throat. "Dishonesty isn't nice, Holly. You're right."

"Thank you," said Holly, in the tone of someone who has finally been heard.

"In fact, it's despicable. But it's not Vân Uớc who is dishonest. It's you, isn't it?"

262

Holly looked uncomfortable. "No."

Michael pressed on, pinning Holly like an insect with the intensity of his look. "You stole the tag Vân Ước told you about. You took the evidence that she was telling the truth. You set her up. You deliberately tried to make her look bad in front of everyone else."

Because Michael so rarely spoke to the gathered masses, everyone was listening, just for the novelty value. So everyone saw Holly's face go pale under its tan and then flush bright red.

Michael smiled grimly. "The CCTV has its uses after all. Did you know there's one by the lockers?"

All eyes were still on Holly.

"Why would you do that to Vân Ước?" asked Billy.

"For a laugh," Holly said.

"You have a very ugly sense of humor," someone said. It was Vân Ước. She'd said it out loud! She was gathering some looks of approval.

Holly walked out.

Michael wasn't looking happy, but grimly satisfied.

"Thank you," said Vân Ước.

"Yeah, good work, man," said Billy. "Did you hack the CCTV file?"

Michael smiled enigmatically. "I didn't need to." He looked at Vân Ước. "Holly knew what was written on the tag, but you never told her what it said. I was just waiting for the right opportunity to denounce her."

Vân Ước wondered about the coincidence of weather; rain was the only reason Michael was putting up with the common room noise to eat his lunch on this particular day. What would she be feeling right now, and what would be the consequences, had the day been fine and her confession heard? Not only had he saved her from possible expulsion, he'd also managed to exonerate her from Holly's false charges in such a satisfyingly public way.

And for once, she'd managed to speak up.

• • •

She met Billy on the way out of school, after his session with the principal and Ms. King, and he walked a little way with her, debriefing.

Michael had got off lightly. He had a perfect record. He wasn't a natural fit at school, but he put up with everything either stoically or, where possible, by taking the absentminded path of least resistance, not interested in exercising teenage rebellion, exerting his preference not to take part in certain activities in ways that were acceptable to the school. He was reprimanded. He apologized with apparent sincerity, and left. No punishment. She was touched that he had exploited his perfect record for her sake.

But Billy was another story. He was way down at the other end of the behavior scale. In fact, he was Mr. Final Warning. He was disrespectful to teachers. This wasn't his first elaborate prank, and, according to Dr. Dryden, Billy had to learn that these pranks he considered to be so funny wasted valuable time and upset people.

He had been late more than a few times to rowing training

as well as missing the lunchtime ergo today, and had already been the subject of conversation between Dr. Dryden and the rowing coach. They weren't prepared to be lenient anymore.

Billy's behavior, according to Dr. Dryden, was defiant, complacent, and arrogant. Didn't Billy realize that there were other able rowers who were very motivated to make the first eight, who would turn up punctually, who would respect their fellow crew members?

"I'm so fucking sick of everything," said Billy. "I just want the world to go away so I can spend some time with you."

This was not comforting, nor was it romantic, as he had perhaps intended it to be, and it made resolving the wish investigation even more pressing. What if his "fascination" with her was at the expense of all the things that were formerly and should perhaps still be really important to him, like rowing? Was she unwittingly warping his worldview? Messing with his whole life trajectory? She didn't want that kind of power.

"What did you say to Dr. Dryden?"

"Well—I probably shouldn't have said what I said."

She had to push him.

"Dryden threatened me. He said if I put even one hair out of place, I'd be off the crew."

"And?"

"And I said, *Consider me off the crew, then, because odds are I'll have more than one hair out of place before too long.*"

"And?"

"And then I didn't say, *Fuck you and fuck school*—there's restraint for you. I just walked out."

"You didn't!"

"It felt…great."

"But you *love* rowing."

"I have loved it, but I've been thinking about it since we talked on Friday—and, no kidding, this feels like a weight off. It's just got so intense. Too important. And the Brown thing— sure, kudos, but do I really want *years* more of it? Right now— no. So, stand back and wait for the shit to start pouring down."

"Did he call your parents?"

"He will have spoken to them by the time I get home." Billy pulled the buzzing phone out of his pocket. "Yeah, right on cue: Mum, Dad, and no doubt they'll get Harry—my sister—to call, too, but she's in Boston, so I've got a few hours' reprieve. Full family disapproval coming my way." Billy kissed Vân Ước. "Wish me luck."

"Luck. Will you call me?"

"Yep."

He walked off, looking back with a rueful smile. She blew him a quick kiss and walked home alone, chewing it all over. She, enthralled with Billy though she was, had no wish for the world to go away. She was just hoping he could be fitted into the few spaces she had between all her other commitments. Maybe there'd be a time, sometime, when the other stuff would be finished and, sure, then she'd happily see the world disappear for a while.

45

She'd been memorizing French verbs out loud after dinner, so her parents wouldn't register when she answered her phone to talk through stage 2 of the Billy saga: The Family Disapproves.

Billy said his mother was mostly "very disappointed" and it was left to his father to use the heavy artillery: *Do you realize what you're giving up? Do you have any idea how many boys would kill for this opportunity? How dare you presume to walk away from a job half done! Are you a winner or a quitter? You'll never achieve anything in life if you're complacent about the head start you've had. How do you think this is going to look on your school record? If you had any strength of character, you'd stick with it. You made a commitment and now you're letting everyone down. You owe the principal, your coach, and your crew an apology. It's hard to recognize you're my son.*

"That's all so . . . harsh, and critical."

"I've had versions of the talk before, but it's the angriest I've ever seen my father."

"What about your sister? What does she think?"

"She was cranky because my mother's call woke her up. She thinks I should take the path of least resistance, put up with it till the end of school, and decide then."

"That sounds like okay advice."

"Only I've already decided. Jeez, it's not like I'm dropping out of school or using heroin."

"Your dad's reaction does sound extreme."

"Yeah, for someone so smart, he's really dumb. It just boils down to *why can't I control you anymore?*" He sounded tired. "They're so into me achieving *their* goals."

"They just want you to be successful, as they are. My parents want me to be successful, as they are not. When I tell them the artist plan there will be a tsunami of disapproval. They want me to study medicine, too."

She could hear Billy smile. "We could run a course."

"*Letting your parents down in ten easy steps.* Are they punishing you?"

"My dad's giving me time to think it all over. He still thinks I'll fold. And that'll happen when—never."

"Wow, I don't get why it's hard for him to recognize you as his son."

Billy laughed. "Okay, we're both stubborn arseholes. I'm

guessing I'll be grounded for a while. So that'll make two of us who aren't allowed out."

"I was kind of joking with the whole date-night-the-final-frontier, but..."

"We'll find a way."

The English portal, open on her screen, stepped up with a possible solution. "Do you know when we could do it? Maybe?"

"When?"

"That notice we got today—the film screening."

"Genius."

"Good night."

"Night."

She smiled as she hung up. As long as she could get Jess on board for a little extra insurance, her parents should let her go on a school-sanctioned outing.

46

"Just taking these into Jess for her camp," said Vân Ước the next morning as she walked past her mother, holding up a pair of hiking boots and a rain jacket.

"Come back for some breakfast. I'm making *bánh ăn sáng.*"

"Is there one for Jess?"

"Yes. Okay."

Her stomach rumbled at the thought of her mother's egg *bánh ăn sáng*—yeasty buns from Liên Luu, filled with scrambled eggs with crispy shallots, chili, and heaps of fresh coriander.

Vân Ước knocked and walked in just as Jess's mother was leaving for work.

"Thanks, Vân Ước," she said, looking at the gear. "She's still asleep. Go in and get her to wake up!"

She walked into Jess's bedroom. "Hey, wake up—it's camp day."

Jess groaned. She was never a morning person at the best of times, and on a day that her class was heading off for a two-day camp for bonding and hiking in the bush, she was even less enthusiastic than usual.

"I need a favor," Vân Ước said.

"What?"

"Come to see a film with me, so my parents feel okay about me going?"

"What movie?"

"It's a filmed National Theatre production of *King Lear*, screening at the Nova."

Jess was properly awake now. She got up and headed for the kitchen as she processed the request.

"I guess."

"Only, I won't be there for the actual film."

"Too early for mysterious talk."

"Because I'll be with Billy. Pleeease say yes."

Jess thought about it. "I could really do with seeing a production of *Lear*—sure, I'll go."

"I love you."

"I know it. Do you want coffee?"

"Come back with me, we've got eggy *bánh ăn sáng*."

That woke Jess up properly. She went back to her room, grabbed a robe, slippers, and keys, and followed Vân Ước back to her place for breakfast.

47

Twelve Balmain Street, Abbotsford, was inked in Vân Ước's diary for after school Thursday, witchy-wish-writer-teacher visit, take two.

The street wasn't so deserted this time. As she pressed the doorbell, Vân Ước got a suspicious once-over from the next-door neighbors who were throwing a bird net over their fruit-laden fig tree.

Ms. Bartloch opened the door after one flat bing-bong chime from inside. She was retro-outfitted again; today, she was channeling Lois Lane, and carrying a big work bag—just arrived home, or about to go out.

"Hello." She was clearly surprised to see Vân Ước.

Now or never. "Ms. Bartloch, I looked you up in the directory. I'm sorry to disturb you."

"Remind me—you're from the year-eleven class at Crowthorne?"

She nodded. "I'm the one who lost the little glass vial—at the beginning of term? Sorry about that. My name's Vân Ước." She'd rehearsed this, but couldn't bring herself to deliver the next line, which was, *Has anything unusual ever happened with the small wish vial before?*

The old dudes were there, talking softly: *She's standing there like a complete dummy/Good for her for coming back, though/ Not if she can't say what she needs to.*

"The most unusual things happen with that..." Ms. Bartloch was rummaging through her very large bag. She put it down on the veranda's cushion-strewn bench, lifted out the box of prompts, and from the box pulled the vial. It was the one: the same handwritten word, *wish*, in the same spidery writing, trapped within.

"But—I couldn't find it that day in class. I really searched."

Ms. Bartloch shrugged. "I guess someone else must have picked it up and returned it to the box."

Vân Ước said, "You don't think—I mean..." She laughed at the sheer ridiculousness of what she was about to say, then stopped, shaking her head. "No, don't worry, it's too silly..."

"If you're about to ask me, does this little thing have the power to grant a wish, you're not the first student to ask, and my answer is..." She looked straight at Vân Ước. "My answer is, who knows?"

"Really?"

"Put it this way. Officially, I don't believe in magic. But a couple of times in England I've stayed in big old houses, and when there's a bedroom with a big old wardrobe, I step in and I put my hand right up to the back of it. I'm checking for fur coats, snow, and pine needles." She frowned. "And, as I say it, I realize I no longer seem rational."

"Have you read *Jane Eyre*?"

"More than once."

"What do you make of Jane Eyre hearing Mr. Rochester calling her name?"

"Exactly—you couldn't meet a more sensible character, right? But she heard something."

"I rely on Jane, but she is fictional," said Vân Ước.

"Hey, some of the best people I know are fictional." Ms. Bartloch held the wish vial out. "Take it. Try again, and see how it goes." She gave Vân Ước the most reassuring of smiles. The smile said, *I don't think you're crazy, I don't think it's magic, but I wish you luck.*

"I shouldn't," Vân Ước said as her fingers closed around the vial. "I already lost it once."

"And yet here it is, finding you." Ms. Bartloch zipped up her bag, slung it back over her shoulder, and said, "No big deal. I know the tree they grow on."

Holding the wish vial, Vân Ước watched as Ms. Bartloch went back inside the house; she felt 50 percent stupid, 50 percent hopeful, and 100 percent terrified.

She slipped the vial into the side pocket of her dress and zipped it.

Jess was right, the phrasing of the wish was going to take some figuring out. None of the re-wishes she'd come up with would do. She didn't want to accidentally wish for something dumb, as fairy-tale wishers always do, and end up with a sausage for a nose.

She shook her head and seriously wondered if she should be making an appointment with Dr. Chin to get a referral to a psychiatrist.

● ● ●

When she got home, she was still worry-deep in wish land, and didn't even notice the group of boys in the playground area again until she heard the catcalling whistle.

"Wouldn't mind a piece of that," said Nick.

She stopped as though she'd been smacked. "I just saw your mum down Albert Street, Nick. And your little sister."

She walked right over to the boys and spoke in a loud, clear voice. She hardly recognized herself. And it was obvious that neither did they. "How would you like someone telling your mum or your sisters they wouldn't mind *a piece of that*?"

The boys were shifting about uncomfortably, not looking at her.

"Huh? Didn't hear you."

"Just sayin', you're looking hot, girl," Nick mumbled.

"Well, you don't get to judge me. I'm not here for your assessment."

"It's just a fucken compliment," Nick said.

"No, it's sexual harassment. And I'm sick of it." She made eye contact with each boy. "And don't call me 'girl.' I have a name, and you've all known it since we were five. You owe me an apology. You're better than this. Most of you," she said, saving her harshest look for Nick. "And, come *on*, you guys, you're just as bad as he is if you let him say that stuff. Tell him to cut it out if he talks like that to me, or to any other girl."

A couple of mumbled *sorry*s came her way from the swings and monkey bars. And Matthew said, "Nick?" with an accompanying persuasive shove.

"Okay," Nick said. "Sorry. Jeez."

"All right," she said. "Just remember. Have some respect."

She kept her composure until she was inside the building, but it was impossible to resist a few tap-dance steps on her way to the elevator to express the effervescence she felt at finally speaking up.

Jane would definitely approve.

48

…gentle reader may you never feel what I then felt…

When she unlocked the door and walked in, she sobered at once, seeing her mother's somber face. Her mother sat her down.

"You have asked to hear more, *con*. But I've never wanted to infect you with my sadness."

"I want to know your story. Whatever you want to tell me."

It seemed that once the floodgates had opened, it was easier for her mother to keep talking than to remain silent.

● ● ●

As her mother spoke, Vân Ước felt the reverberation of so many firsthand accounts she'd read over the years.

They escaped on their third attempt—her mother, her father, and her aunt. It was 1980. Her mother was twenty-one. The boat they were on, like many commissioned for this work, was not a particularly safe vessel; it was built for rivers, not for the open sea.

Overcrowding. Insufficient, cramp-inducing space per person. Minimal belongings. Enough water and food for a few days. Ridiculous expectations. Faith. Fear.

When the engine broke down after three days, no one was surprised. With any luck they would drift or catch a tow to land within another day. But another day passed; they were becalmed. Another day, and things were getting ugly. The scorching sun and calm, turquoise waters would surely kill them. They sat, by now, in a swill of excrement, bilge water, and fear.

At first babies were crying and could not be comforted, then they lost the energy to cry. There was very little water left. Her mother was sixteen weeks pregnant. Her father and her aunt, Hoa Nhung, were looking after her mother as well as they could, but she was dehydrated and exhausted from vomiting. Fellow travelers, crammed into the stinking vessel like sardines, resented the water, fed to her sip by sip by Vân Ước's father, that she reliably threw up.

They ran out of everything except the hope-despair that had put them on board in the first place.

Her mother remembered looking up into the pitiless sky and, because she felt sure she was going to die, wishing what she guessed were probably pointless wishes, but wishing anyway. She knew she should have been praying this close to the end, but she'd lost heart, after all she had seen and survived, first in Vietnam, and then on this journey—for nothing, in the end; she'd lost faith. So she sent wishes up into that lidless blue eye. *Baby be safe, baby be strong, baby grow up without fear, without hunger. Be free. Let me die, let my baby live.*

When someone spotted another boat in the water, relief washed over them. This was good luck, a chance that they would reach their destination, after all. The air was briefly celebratory. But as the boat drew closer, they recognized it as a vessel carrying Thai pirates. There was an outpouring of anxiety. There was no escape. In fact, they needed the boat to approach them; some water and some help with the engine was their only hope for survival. In a scramble and panic, children were taken below and hidden. Some of the women started crying and screaming: they knew their likely fate.

Her father and Hoa Nhung hacked off her mother's hair, and wiped oil from the engine room over her face and hands. Her father took off his shirt and put it on her mother. She was barely conscious of what they were doing, but she knew what was happening when the pirates tied the two boats together and took a group of women, including her sister, onto their boat.

Her mother thinks she must have appeared to be a dirty little boy; none of the pirates looked twice at her.

The women were brought back on board the next day. The whole boat was silent with grief for what the women had suffered. The men were ashamed that they had been powerless to stop it. The pirates took everything of value they could find, including the gold teeth of five men, which they pulled out with pliers.

The next day they crossed paths with another boat, were given food and water and help fixing the engine.

The day after that her mother miscarried, and their boat puttered into sight of land.

People were so relieved to see the beaches stretch out before them that they jumped overboard. Out of their depth. Still. Many were unable to swim. But those who could swim helped those who couldn't.

Vân Ước imagined the shapes they made in the water, stars and circles and waving lines as they gathered, each to the other, making sure all were safe, all were included. Such generosity after the unimaginable bleakness.

• • •

This, then, has been the heart of her mother's misery: she had never forgiven herself for what happened to her sister.

"Is this why we don't ever see my auntie, Hoa Nhung?"

"I am as guilty as if it happened yesterday. She could have saved herself, cut her own hair, made her own face dirty, but instead she saved me."

"She wanted to help you look after the baby."

Her mother had tears streaming down her face. "It was all for nothing. I couldn't save my baby, either."

"Mama, nobody could have made things better. I'm sure my auntie told you that, too."

"We never spoke of what happened."

Vân Ước struggled to squash the giddy relief of finally being told something, no matter how heartbreaking. It was no worse than her anxious speculations. And, finally, she had one true story to fix upon.

She tried to imagine her mother's burden, the weight of unspoken misery and shame, for all those years. She knew it was one way that people coped. They suffered all the pain and depredations of the journey, a journey for which they had forsaken everything. They ruled a line under it, and turned to the next task. If they were lucky, they survived. If they were lucky, they were offered asylum in Australia, or America, or Canada. If they were lucky, they arrived, and were eventually reunited with some family members. They looked forward. They learned to get by in a new language. They got jobs. They got on with their lives. They were so lucky. So they believed.

It was the most sustained talking Vân Ước had ever heard from her mother. They sat together on the sofa, and her mother let Vân Ước put an arm around her. She allowed Vân Ước to hug her, without pushing her away. And Vân Ước heard herself make the soothing sounds that parents make to children waking from nightmares. *There, there, it's all right. It's all right, now.*

49

Because Jess was away at camp and they couldn't have movie night, Vân Ước was officially home alone after school and homework club on Friday, so she finally agreed that Billy could come and visit her. He figured he could get away with a "run" while he was grounded.

Her parents went downstairs at quarter past six to be collected by Bác Bảo for their regular Friday dinner.

At six thirty the buzzer sounded.

She looked around while she waited for Billy to come up.

The old dudes did a quick inventory for her: *Vinyl-covered sofa and chairs with a split in the arm of one chair mended with insulation tape/Plastic "lace" cloth on the table, large-screen TV disproportionate to the living space/Small kitchen, upright cooker with electric coil cooktop/He's going to be so impressed/At least she's hidden those horrible photos of herself as a child.*

She couldn't help thinking of the scene in *Pretty in Pink* where Andie said to Blane that she didn't want him to see where she lived. And she lived in a house!

She tried to make herself feel okay by remembering that she seemed to be in the bubble with Billy. Nothing she did or said or was could be wrong. She felt the familiar excitement battling it out with sickness at the whole idea of the wish, more so now that she had the small glass vial, well hidden under papers in the top drawer of her desk.

Billy knocked. She led him in; they went straight into her room. Her pretty room. She'd decorated it over the years with thrift-shop treasures and it was a space that pleased her every time she walked in. Billy was drawn straight to her window.

"That's so cool," he said. The late-afternoon light was shining through the sixty-seven crystal decanter stoppers she had suspended at different heights with fishing line from the underside top of the window frame, forming a sparkling "curtain" over the entire window. She had rigged up a frame of wood inside the aluminum frame, allowing her to arrange the installation.

"People drop decanters, so lots of lonely stoppers find their way into junk baskets at thrift shops. Or they used to."

As they stood, color-washed in the flickering rainbows, Billy leaned down to kiss her, with an *mmm* sigh that sounded as though he'd settled somewhere extremely comfortable, and she responded for a dazzling, drowning minute before breaking away.

"Sorry, I meant to say when you came in, I can't do this, can't do anything—not here."

"Are you sure?" Billy kissed her once more.

She was tempted, but resolved. "It's too thin—the space between the front door and here. I don't feel safe."

Billy flopped down on her bed with a joke-groan of anguish. "You're killing me."

"I know. But we can't."

Billy sat up. "I can't stay for long anyway. I'm supposed to be running. So, what do you want to do on Sunday?"

"I don't know." Vân Ước sat next to him on the bed. "I've never been on a date before, so I'm expecting you to do most of the work here."

"We'll have about three and a half hours. It's one of the longest films in existence. And I know one thing I want to do," he said, smiling. "I'm taking you somewhere secret."

"Where?"

"Duh. It's a secret."

"I've got somewhere I'd like to take you, too."

"Where?"

"Seeing as we're playing it like this: also *secret*. But it involves food," she said.

"Does that sound like a couple of hours?"

"Yeah, so maybe we can do one more thing—I'm happy to just be together, alone."

"We can walk."

"I can hold your hand. And I've got another food thing. We

can do that last; it's right near the Nova. Are we picking Jess up there after the movie?"

"Yeah. How are things going at your place, poor you?"

"Arctic. My parents hate my guts. The hatred will culminate in our family 'conference' with Dryden, when my shitty attitude will be dissected and spread out on a table for all to see and despise. Hatred should diminish with time, with a likely thaw coinciding with footy season." He stopped making light of it. "What freaks them out is the possibility that I've really stopped playing along with their whole dumb plan. Will it snowball? Will I remember to be a famous doctor, or has that also dropped off my list?" He gave her an apologetic look. "And for some reason, they associate it with you."

"*I'm* a bad influence?"

"I tried to make it clear you are the opposite of a bad influence, but I guess you were the only thing my mother could pinpoint that had changed in my life."

That stung; she hadn't really registered that she wanted the approval of Billy's family until she felt the unfairness of having earned their disapproval, and knew that it attached to her being socially unacceptable in their eyes. "If only they knew—I would have to be the most study-hard girlfriend you could find."

"I told them all that." Billy flopped backward on the bed and pulled Vân Ước down beside him. She started to sit up, but he said, "Just lie here with me." He resettled his arm around her more comfortably, kissing her chastely on the earlobe before closing his eyes. "Tell me something to make me feel better."

Make him feel better.

Make *him* feel better?

She thought about what it meant to be considered a bad influence, just because she was born outside a tiny social circle.

She looked up at the ceiling and thought about what her own family had survived, still so new and raw to her.

She thought about Debi's family during the Second World War, what they'd been through in the Warsaw Ghetto, then in hiding; how all had been persecuted, and most had died.

She thought about families in Gaza during 2014, when nowhere in the city was safe from Israeli airstrikes, not even schools, not even hospitals.

She thought about the schoolgirls kidnapped in Chibok, Nigeria, still not rescued.

She thought about the family from South Sudan who just moved in down the hallway, and the slash scars all over the father's face and neck.

She thought about the millions of dispossessed people jammed into refugee camps all over the world.

The relentless relativity she applied to her own life bowed her down. Studying hard? Practicing hard? Not as bad as living under the oppression of the communists. Tired after school? Not as bad as risking your life on a leaky boat. Feeling lonely? Try saying good-bye to your family, expecting never to see them again.

It wasn't as though her parents had ever said those things explicitly—it was enough to know it. She was nearly seventeen; she was perfectly capable of punishing herself. Inherited oppression and deprivation and fear was a gut-clench she never got to release.

Make *him* feel better?

She calmed herself down.

His problem was real, to him, right now.

She glanced sideways, ready to relent and kiss him, but his breathing was regular and deep; he was asleep. She watched his beautiful face in repose and tried not to feel jealous of this boy who'd never had cause to compare his daily woes with anything worse than other privileged people's daily woes.

It would take guts to hold the line and really step away from rowing. It was clear that neither his parents nor the school had accepted his decision as final. They still expected him to grovel, toe the line, and get back in the eight.

He'd be in free fall after so much scheduling, and planning, and control. Saying good-bye to so many desirable, known outcomes. His ancestors with their own ideas of duty and respect and obedience would frown on him; outnumbering him, they'd hurl their degrees and their trophies at him through time and space.

But he'd made up his mind. He was turning his back on this particular chapter of public "winning." Saying good-bye to the security of consensus status. That was pretty brave.

She kissed him awake.

● ● ●

Walking Billy to the elevator, she saw the stained concrete floor, the low ceiling, and the exposed pipes of the hallway with fresh eyes. She glanced at him; was he judging her surroundings as harshly as she was? Didn't look that way. All he seemed to notice was her. He blew her a kiss as the elevator door closed.

She had left a clear half hour between him leaving and her parents' return to be sure that they would not cross paths. Even so, she went out into the hallway and reentered the apartment sniffing (twice) to see if she could detect any telltale Billy smell. She went into her room, smelled her pillow—she was happy to detect a tiny hint of him there—and found a single strand of his hair, which she removed, screwed up into a piece of paper, and disposed of with forensic care.

50

Sunday afternoon dragged with oboe practice, math home-work, and occasional pillow sniffs until it was time for Vân Ước and Jess to leave.

Because of the letter she'd brought home from Ms. Norton, strongly advising that all students attend the Nova screening of *King Lear*, it had, for once, been ridiculously easy to get a few free hours. Jess also persuaded her parents that she would benefit from seeing the film, and that made Vân Ước's leave pass secure. The girls were even allowed to travel there and back together, although Vân Ước had agreed to text her father when they got on the tram to come home so he could meet them at the tram stop.

Billy was also greenlit for the screening, despite being grounded.

One tram into the city, another along Swanston Street to Carlton, and then a few blocks' walk to the movie theater.

"Look at you," said Jess. "It's like there's a little light switched on inside."

That was exactly how it felt: as though she were illuminated, suffused with light, and yet, in seeming contradiction, sharply focused. Love adrenaline. *Love?* Oh, dear. But it didn't feel like the wrong word. This wasn't good. An old unrequited crush was manageable, something she understood, a thing that knew its place in the world. Love? That was another thing entirely. She stopped walking.

"Now what?" asked Jess. "I said the wrong thing? There's no little light?"

"There's a light." Walking again. "I wonder if that's where 'carrying a torch for someone' comes from."

"Nuh, that seems more likely a pre-electricity thing. Dragon-fighting era," said Jess.

As they approached the movie theater, Billy was already there, leaning against a wall, next to . . . his father.

Billy saw her, but carefully wasn't acknowledging her. She detoured Jess into Brunetti's. "We're going to browse pastries for a few minutes."

"Suits me." They had barely finished admiring the first display case of miniature cannoli when Billy came in.

"Sorry, he was sticking to me like glue. Making sure I went into the movie theater."

"Which is where I'm going," said Jess. "I don't want to miss the ads. Have fun, kids."

"Thanks, Jess," said Vân Ước. "Meet you back here when the movie gets out."

"Actually—we'll be there," said Billy, pointing to the gelati counter at the back of the long cafe. "After the movie. If you'll let me buy you an ice cream to say thanks."

"You say *thank you* with ice cream?" said Jess. She looked at Vân Ước. "Any doubts I had are officially gone." She smiled mischievously and walked off.

"What doubts?" Billy asked Jess's back. "What doubts did she have?" he asked Vân Ước. "Why would anyone have doubts about me?"

"I think you've answered your own question," said Vân Ước. She tilted her head to one side, as though considering exactly how to best express it. "It's that touch of the arrogant prat..."

"You don't think that about me anymore. Now you know me..." Billy said, holding her hand.

"Now that I know you, I think you're okay." Her smile was brimming over, totally blowing the moderate impression that *okay* should, ideally, convey.

They walked along Lygon Street, past the restaurants, mostly Italian places, and clothes shops, mostly high-street chains, and cut back to Swanston Street, where they jumped on a tram.

"What if we see someone?"

Billy leaned in and kissed her. "I couldn't care less."

Vân Ước sat up straight. "Me neither." She tried to mean it. "Where are we going?"

"I already told you: secret special place."

When they got off at the stop near Billy's house, she was surprised, slightly alarmed, and excited. Had he managed to empty his house? Were they just going to spend some quality time in his room? They certainly wouldn't get anything else done, if that was his plan.

But they headed onto a street one over from Billy's. About halfway down that street he led her along a bluestone-paved alleyway that turned a corner and, rather than leading to another alleyway of back fences and garages, opened onto a tiny street tucked into a hidden parallel zone between the two streets she knew.

Billy smiled in satisfaction at her delight. The houses were Victorian-era terraces, some single- and some two-story. Light glowed in glimpses of windows through hedge-lined wrought-iron fences. Only about fifteen houses sat on either side of the street, an odd little subdivision carved from large original allotments. But what gave the street its otherworldliness was the dark-leafed orange trees that lined it, almost meeting overhead.

Walking along the narrow roadway, enveloped in the sharp orange-blossom scent—citrus, astringent, sweet, and deep—was like being in a dream. This could not be real. Vân Ước stopped, closed her eyes, stretched out her arms and spun in a full circle. They continued along slowly as the dusk began to gather, hands loosely linked. At the other end of the street, Billy stopped Vân Ước, covered her eyes gently and turned her around. When he took his hand away she opened her eyes and saw the sign—Atienza Lane.

"What's the story?"

"People who live around here come and pick the oranges in season, and Mel asked about it one day. She and I spoke to a woman who used to live right there…" He pointed to the second-last house across the road from where they were standing. "One of the original families in the street came from Seville, where there are, apparently—I haven't been there—heaps of orange trees planted along the city streets. The family offered to supply trees for the whole street if each family would look after the tree outside their house. And people did. It's not like it's a council-approved tree, but this is so tucked away here, nobody official noticed, or if they did, they turned a blind eye. And the family loved it, because the street smelled like home to them. You know—once the trees grew up."

Vân Ước smiled. "They put down roots."

"And—last bit of intel—they're Seville orange trees; the fruit is bitter and rough-skinned, but great for marmalade. According to Mel. Whose marmalade is the best."

"I love it."

"And it seemed like a good place to kiss you."

"That's what it smells like."

"Like…?" He kissed her.

"Like a kiss feels, when you're on the very edge of falling in love," she whispered, then shut her eyes, and fell.

● ● ●

They walked across the river on the footbridge, along Birrarung Marr to the riverbank directly across from the rowing sheds, to the hawkers market—pop-up stalls selling food from Vietnam, Laos, Malaysia, China…It was the last one for the season, while daylight saving was still in place and the evenings were long.

She looked around and spotted Henry's stall. There was a queue waiting for food. She waved to Sherry, who was serving, and saw Gary's red bandanna. He was cooking satays on the compact grill. Henry was standing around looking good. She took Billy over.

"I'm officially at a movie, or I'm dead—so please don't blow my cover. This is Billy."

They shook hands, smiled, and *hey, man*-ed each other.

"Let me grab you something to eat. What would you like?"

"You choose something for us," she said, adding, to Billy, "It's all delicious."

When Henry reappeared with two loaded noodle boxes, she reached into her bag for her wallet; she was giving herself carte blanche with the contingency fund tonight. This might be a oncer, she figured, so she should live it up. Billy put his hand over her hand, reaching into his pocket. Henry put up his hand. "It's on me. Worker's bonus."

In each box was a cucumber, vermicelli, and mint salad with peanuts and fine shreds of chili, two mini sticky red-bean dumplings, and a bunch of chicken satays, fragrant from the grill.

"You are awesome," said Vân Ước.

Henry smiled in agreement.

They found an empty bench under a plane tree. An illuminated party boat cruised along the river, rippling colored lights across the water; people on the boat were dancing. Vân Ước could hear floating fragments of a band playing farther along the riverbank. It sounded like the Darjeelings.

They ate the delicious food in silence, punctuated only by Billy's satisfied groans of *omigod that's amazing* pleasure as he ate. Vân Ước was amused to note that these groans had a lot in common with the groans that accompanied him kissing her, as though she, too, was *omigod that's amazing* delicious.

She'd read somewhere once that it was likely that someone who truly appreciated the sensual pleasure of food would also be a good lover. Based on that assessment, Billy's potential was excellent.

When it was time to head back to Carlton, they decided to cut through the city taking only alleyways, if they could. After skirting the back of Federation Square, they alley-walked the whole grid north, right up to La Trobe Street, starting at Oliver Lane and finishing on Exploration Lane. They crossed over to the Carlton Gardens, stopping for an irresistible—despite her aversion to public affection—lamp-lit embrace.

Billy wrapped his arms around her. Standing so close together their softness, hardness, arcs, declivities touched and met with a sense of perfect fit. He felt...right. She kissed him, shadowed by a tree, and fell, lost and new, into the vivid response her body had to his.

"Do you know what's weird?" he asked.

"My heartbeat accelerates when I kiss you, even though I'm standing still?"

He shook his head. "I never knew falling in love would be this—easy."

"Me neither." She felt floaty-dazed from the impact.

"It's like I'm addicted to you, and it happened like that." He snapped his fingers.

And here was the familiar pang of doubt—her awareness of exactly how sudden was the onset of Billy's love—but she put it firmly out of her mind. This was their date, a couple of uninterrupted hours together that might never be repeated, and she was going to enjoy it, even if it meant wearing blinders.

"It should come with a warning label, like habituating pharmaceuticals," he said as they hurried across the road into Grattan Street.

It was only half an hour before they had to meet Jess, and Vân Ước had one more thing she wanted to do.

● ● ●

They stopped outside Readings. "Okay, it doesn't quite compare to the orange blossoms, but this is one of my favorite smells."

Walking inside, she inhaled deeply. Fresh books. "My plan is we separate and choose a book for each other. Five minutes, then meet back here at the counter."

"I can bear five minutes apart, I guess." Billy turned away after kissing her softly on the lips, as though parting for a longer time. The girl behind the counter gave Vân Ước a really nice smile, a smile that would be *aww*, if it turned itself into a word.

They wandered deeper into the shop. She went first to check for copies of *Jane Eyre* on the shelves. Prospective readers should have access at all times. Tick, three copies.

She went from the Bs to the Ms, looking for the book she'd decided to buy Billy. *Flypaper* by Robert Musil. She took the slim volume from the shelf and dipped into it, confirming it was as she remembered, and wondered what Billy was choosing for her. She could see his head a few stacks away.

At the front counter he revealed his choice, *The Life of Charlotte Brontë* by Elizabeth Gaskell. The perfect boy had chosen the perfect book. She looked into his eyes. *I feel akin to him,—I understand the language of his countenance and movements... I have something in my brain and heart, in my blood and nerves, that assimilates me mentally to him.*

They smiled, kissed, paid, exchanged books, and crossed the road to meet up with Jess.

● ● ●

As she and Jess rode home on the tram, Jess was full of having met and sat next to Eliza, from Vân Ước's class. She'd talked to Eliza, spent the intermission with Eliza, shared Maltesers with Eliza.

"So what's she like?" Jess asked. "Eliza."

"Nice. She runs. She's a fanatically good runner."

Jess smiled enigmatically. "Yeah. I'm going for a run with her on Saturday."

Vân Ước looked at her sideways. "You don't run."

297

"I do now. Does she like girls?"

Vân Ước shrugged. "No sign of being into boys. Might this be the end of the in-waiting period?"

"I don't know," said Jess. "A girl can dream. A girl can go for a run with another girl. How was the date?"

Vân Ước filled Jess in. "And then—you were there for the last bit."

"For my money, you can't end a date on a better note than a double cone of dark chocolate and mulberry gelati," said Jess reflectively. "And the way he looked at you when he said good night at the tram stop..."

"And now that's it. Good-bye, happiness." Vân Ước slumped back in her seat. "I think this is the slough of despond. I'm in it, right now. Or it's in me."

Jess gave her the classic *puh-leeze* look: a soft center of incredulity, coated in get-a-grip. "One, I don't think it is the end. And, two, you've never needed a boy to be happy, and you don't now."

"He's my ultimate mew, without a doubt in the world. I have a strong preference at this particular point in time that I get to kiss him some more. And if I don't, my immediate, day-to-day happiness quotient will be diminished. Severely."

"Fair point."

"What would you do? Real answer."

"Me? I'd ride the wish train."

"Really?"

"Sure! Particularly because I don't believe it. But you? You're not going to be happy with that. You need to dredge the misery. You need to unwish the good times. Your problem is"—Jess smiled and bumped her shoulder sideways into Vân Ước fondly—"asking *what would freakin' Jane do?* It's given you an excess of honesty. You're too ethical for your own good."

"I've always been honest. It predates Jane."

"She made it worse. Hey, maybe you secretly don't want the good times. Did you ever think of that, my cray friend?"

"I want the good times."

As they were getting off the tram, Jess paused, puzzled, and said, "Isn't it early for orange trees to be blossoming?"

51

Curled up in her bedroom chair that night, Vân Ước thought about boat trips, putting down roots, bitter marmalade, and what makes home home. How many times do your feet have to press down on a path before they make an imprint, before pieces of soul start sticking? What makes us belong in the place we call home? Who had said that someone you love must be buried in a land before it could be considered to be your home?

That morning, she had knelt on the rough asphalt footpath, meticulously brushing away the grit encircling the silver disk she was photographing, knowing she must look odd, but she didn't care; everyone around here knew her; these were her streets, hers to walk, hers to photograph, to transform. Her very DNA was somewhere in that footpath from childhood skinned knees.

And there was her lightbulb moment for her art portfolio.

It was seductive, the idea of where we walk absorbing us, something of our self being drawn down into the earth with each step we take. What strands might be pulled from our soles as we walk the streets, tired, hopeful, frightened, happy, full of the beauty of what is around us, full of the sorrow of what we are escaping from, or returning to.

It seemed that the paths hummed with the energy pressed into them.

Feeling planted here was the gift her parents gave her.

The gleaming silver chain mail of her footpath disks.

The green and purple jewel-like glass that illuminated the last wave of migrant rag-trade workers, who were eventually superseded by women like her mother, out of the old Flinders Lane workshops, into bedrooms, living rooms, and garages.

The luscious green privilege of the school oval.

Hers, to interpret and offer back to the world. *What it means to me*, she thought, *is what it means to everyone. Belonging where we stand. Knowing that where we stand is home.*

* * *

Some time in the future the big portfolio breakthrough might be a comfort. But now was not that time. What could possibly provide comfort now?

She went, once more, through every detail of the date. One

perfect date is better than no perfect dates. But she would have preferred a few more than one, and would even have settled for a larger number of *meh* dates. Because a *meh* date with Billy would at least have meant more time with him, and, already, in anticipation, she felt sorely cheated on that front.

She took the wish vial from its hiding place, put it on her desk, and sat back on the chair without bothering to put on the light. She slipped down into the realm of full-wallow self-pity—from self-pity at the state of things about to change with Billy, to self-pity that she couldn't really justify her self-pity when she compared her paltry plight to the true peril faced by her mother and her aunt.

Sad and pissed off wove themselves together in one heavy blanket of righteous misery.

She looked at the wish vial, a sliver of silver catching the glow of light that washed soft the city sky at night.

Pick me up. Pick me up. Pick me up.

Shut up.

Her wish phrasing had been idle and careless, forming itself without her having to think about it.

She wasn't about to wish, now, that Billy *didn't* find her fascinating, or prefer her to all other girls.

She wasn't going to wish for something different, and perhaps create a different tangle of problems.

No, Jess had come up with the right word: she was simply going to wish to *unwish* the first wish. That would bring her back to a neutral reality. Back to the time when Billy didn't know who she was, or care who she was, didn't notice her.

Back to the land of true things.

So, that was all she had to do.

Easy.

Plus, she totally didn't believe in it anyway.

Times a thousand.

So.

There was nothing at stake, really.

There was no wish!

It was a simple case of Billy Gardiner loves Vân Ước Phan.

It must be.

Why was it, then, that she'd been sitting here for two hours, in the dark, feeling so bleak, putting off the moment, the simple action, of picking up a small glass vial?

Because even if there were a fraction of a chance that she had, in fact, wished Billy's affection into existence, she was going to miss it like breathing.

She did not want to lose it.

But she wasn't prepared to live with the possibility that his affection was based on a careless wish, i.e., a lie.

Those two things were never going to be reconcilable no matter how long she sat there staring into the deepening night.

She picked up the vial.

She held it for who knew how long.

She held it until it was blood-warm.

With a deep breath that turned into a sob, she unwished the first wish.

Heart racing, she opened her hand. The vial was gone. Again. Misplaced. Disappeared. On her chair. On the floor. Up her sleeve.

Who cared?

The wind screeched and pushed at the windowpanes.

The deed was done.

She walked stiffly the few dark steps across to her bed, fell back onto her pillow, still dressed, and went to sleep crying silent hot tears, in the miserable consciousness of believing the unbelievable, and clenched against the effects of the unwished wish.

52

The morning leaked through her window, poisonous and gray.

Fruit and yogurt. Toast and Vegemite. Despite the bleak new world to which she had awakened, it lifted her spirits to see her mother looking better—lighter. A little smile hovered where usually her customary look was—what was it, exactly? Something more like resignation.

"So, Ma…"

"Vân Ước."

"You were already asleep when I came in?"

"Yes, I slept well."

"Has something happened?"

Her mother was really smiling now. "Last night I spoke to my sister, Hoa Nhung. I called her on the telephone."

"You—really? That's—I'm so happy."

"We spoke for a long time."

"Did you speak about...?"

Her mother nodded. "She saw things differently. She was very pleased that I had not been taken on the boat. She felt proud to protect me. She knew she'd saved me. And she used that feeling—of strength—to help heal."

Vân Ước had always felt the shadow of sadness and guilt for the things, unspoken until now, that her mother suffered. Her mother had felt sad and guilty about her sister's suffering. And about leaving her own mother. No doubt her grandmother felt sad and guilty for sending her daughters away, not really knowing they'd be safe, just hoping. Guilty, too, perhaps, about leaving her own family when she married, to look for better fortune and a new life in the city. How far did it go back? Was it Vân Ước's job to break this chain?

Might things change now that the story had been told?

A secret like that might shut you off.

A secret like that might turn you inward.

A secret like that might stop you from being able to hug your own daughter.

She picked up her lunch, and gave her mother a quick hug. "Bye, Ma. I'm so glad you called my auntie. This is a great step. Do you think she might come and visit us?"

She was ready to talk about it for as long as her mother

wanted to. But her mother just smiled and turned her gently away, in the direction of the door.

"Study hard, *con*. We can talk some more after school."

As the elevator shuddered to the ground floor, she tried not to think of Billy, tried to remind herself that things were okay in the universe at large. Or, at least, in certain small parts of the universe at large. Sure, *she* had a pulverized heart. True, *she* had nothing to look forward to, other than the better part of two years of being, once again, ignored by Billy.

But on the upside, she'd started becoming proper friends with Lou and Michael.

And things were definitely, finally, looking better for her mother. After all that time, some comfort, some truth, some connection.

But, still, it didn't take away the lump in her throat that felt like a stone.

She stepped outside into the cool fingers of autumn, into day one.

Today, *this very day*, would be the worst day; day two—that'd be bad, too, really, really bad, but just a smidge less bad than day one.

She took a firm breath, instructing tears to stay inside.

The number of days it would take before her affection for Billy diminished would surely exceed those left between now and when school finished next year.

She looked up from the path, and headed for the gate.

She blinked. Twice. And again.

A tall, handsome boy with messy blond hair, wearing a Crowthorne Grammar tracksuit, was hurrying toward her.

"You're here."

Billy put a casual arm around her shoulder, but it wasn't enough; he looked at her, eyes still shiny with all they'd shared last night, and enfolded her and her backpack into a proper hug, as though he couldn't get close enough.

It was *as though he still liked her* despite the unwish.

Or, to put it another way: he still liked her?!

Her heart rate doubled and redoubled. He released her, lifted her hand, and kissed the inside of her palm.

"Of course I'm here. We said we'd walk together. How would it be fair for me to deprive you of my company for longer than necessary?"

She did her best to look stern. *"Well, for cool native impudence, and pure innate pride, you haven't your equal,"* she said, calmly enough, though her heart was crazy-pounding...*I stopped, feeling it would not do to risk a long sentence, for my voice was not quite under command.*

Billy recognized that the quote was from *Jane Eyre*. "Remind me—in this exchange, am I Jane or Mr. Rochester?"

"You're Jane."

"Okay. Just so we're straight on that."

• • •

Once upon a long time ago she believed in magic.

But this was looking like a simple case of a girl who liked a

boy who liked her back. And a wish that came true, because—
sometimes they do.

They stopped on the bridge and as she turned him around to
face her, resting her hands on his shoulders and leaning up to
open her lips to the lips of Billy Gardiner, she thought, with a
satisfied sigh, *Reader, I kissed him.*

The Beginning.

ACKNOWLEDGMENTS

Heartfelt thanks to James Adams, Thanh Bùi, Susin Chow, Kaz Cooke; Claire Craig, and the Pan Macmillan team; Cath Crowley, Katelyn Detweiler, Sarah Griffiths, Jill Grinberg, Margaret Gurry, Jeremy Hetzel, Simmone Howell; Farrin Jacobs, Alvina Ling, Maggie Edkins, Victoria Stapleton, Jenny Choy, Jen Graham, Jane Lee, Ruiko Tokunaga, and the rest of the Little, Brown team; Julie Landvogt, Ali Lavau, Olivia McCombe, Giulia McGauran, Monica McGauran, Iola Mathews, Reba Nelson, Diễm Nguyễn, Như-Quỳnh Nguyễn, Cheryl Pientka, Lisa Hop Tran, Vicky Tu, Libby Turner, Michael Wicks, Jamie Wood, Zoe Wood, George Wood.

Thanks to Creative Victoria, and to Writers Victoria and the National Trust for Glenfern Writers' Studios.

An extra curtain call and resounding applause for Thanh Bùi, Diễm Nguyễn, Như-Quỳnh Nguyễn, Lisa Hop Tran, and Vicky Tu, without whose generosity and expertise this book could not have been written.